THE LION TAMER

DAHLIA DONOVAN

To Ron

ALSO BY DAHLIA DONOVAN

THE SIN BIN

The Wanderer
The Caretaker
The Botanist
The Royal Marine
The Unexpected Santa
The Lion Tamer

TRADE ME

Found You

STANDALONE

After the Scrum
Unintentional: North American Edition
The Misguided Confession
One Last Heist

CHAPTER ONE

GRAY

Everything and everyone changes, son. You'd do better to walk on cracked ice on a frozen pond than try to stop life from moving in the direction it wants to go. But if you're unhappy with your path, pick another one—keep picking until you find the right one.

Over thirty years after Old Sam's death, Gray could still hear his words as clear as day. The Colorado rancher had taken him in at fifteen. He'd been a petulant, troubled foster kid everyone else had given up on long ago.

Samuel Baird had served in World War II. In the three years Gray spent on his ranch, Old Sam never once spoke of his years in the Navy, of the horrors he'd seen. *Shell shock.* He'd been sent home from the front with shell shock and missing an arm.

Gray could still remember his social worker telling him this might be his last chance for a good home. *As if the others had been anything but completely fucked up.* But to his immense surprise, Old Sam treated him like a favourite son. The gruff cowboy taught him everything about being a man.

Those few years on the ranch had done more to form Gray as a man than the previous fourteen chaotic and abusive ones spent being thrown from one foster home to the next. Old Sam had taken him in and treated him like a wounded wild animal. He often took in injured creatures, treating them with patient, consistent, reliable care.

He'd adopted Gray—even so far as giving the fifteen-year-old his name.

A new name.

A strong one.

Gray Baird.

He wore it with pride—even if others enjoyed teasing him. *Grey Beard. It's Baird—like bared. Fucking morons.* He saw his name and thought only of the seventy-year-old man who'd made him family.

Old Sam died a month after Gray graduated from high school. He'd wound up joining the military. It seemed the best idea at the time to avoid dealing with the mountain of emotions left at the ranch in Colorado.

And for a time, it had been. Gray grew into himself under the yoke of military service, but he couldn't help wondering if he'd missed the chance to find a new adventure.

Now what?

Gray stood in his bathroom in front of the sink, staring at his steam-blurred reflection. "Well? What are you going to do?"

It had been almost twelve months since his old Navy SEAL buddy, Wyatt Hardy, invited him out to Cardiff to join the Ross & Hardy Security & Protection business. The company had been started by Wyatt and a former British Royal Marine, Hamish Ross. The two men had brought in a selection of retired military colleagues to work together.

At first, the job had seemed a perfect fit for him after retiring first from the Marines, and then from his job as a police chief in Washington State. But Gray quickly discovered that the fast-paced work of providing security for non-profits and offering risk assessment to corporations didn't suit him at all. He had no tolerance for people in suits who refused to listen to someone with actual experience.

Gray turned on the tap for cold water and splashed it up into his face repeatedly until his mind cleared. He scowled at the tired lines etched into his face. "You're getting too damn old to play bodyguard—no matter how noble the cause might be."

Was talking to one's self the first sign of insanity?

Fuck.

Questionable mental health aside, Gray had realised working in private security couldn't be a forever career. His body might be in peak condition but he didn't want to spend more years with high levels of stress. He wanted something to make him happy—not keep him on edge.

Since Christmas the tension had been building in him,

and three weeks into the New Year, Gray had come to the realisation that things had to change. He refused to spend his fifties this unhappy with his day-to-day work life.

In truth, Gray didn't need to work. He'd sold the ranch that Old Sam had willed to him for a decent amount. The money had sat earning interest to provide a retirement for him for over thirty years. He had enough to live comfortably, though maybe not extravagantly.

Gray had never needed much, something he'd also inherited from Sam. Could he be content doing nothing for the rest of his life?

Not a fucking chance.

What do I truly want to spend the next however many years of my life doing? Dodging bullets or taking one for someone else? Sitting on my arse?

What do I love more than anything?

Aside from sex.

Food.

Grabbing a towel to dry his hands and face, Gray strode out of his bathroom. He wrapped the towel around his waist. Owning a restaurant had always been an elusive dream, but was it? Could he leave all of his years of military and police service behind?

While preparing an omelette for himself, Gray sipped his freshly brewed coffee and mulled over the idea. He imagined there would be a host of things to consider before jumping headfirst into the restaurant business. With a deft flick of the pan, he flipped his omelette and went back to contemplating the future.

Am I having a midlife crisis?

Can't be.

I've never had a fucking crisis. Other people have them. I make fucking decisions.

They only closely resemble indecisive moments of doubt.

Deciding to take the metaphorical bull by the horns, Gray grabbed his phone to send a text. He paused a moment to decide which of his bosses would handle the news best. Hamish tended to be less childish than Wyatt.

Right.

Decision made.

Gray: Two things. I quit. Also, who do you know who can help me with opening a restaurant?

Hamish: You can't quit before six in the morning.

Gray: Why the fuck not?

Hamish: It's uncivilised.

Gray: Fucking Brits. I texted you instead of Wyatt to avoid stupidity. Don't make me regret it.

Hamish: Talk to Akash. A bakery isn't a restaurant, but he might have some suggestions for you.

Hamish: Are you going to tell Wyatt that you've abandoned us?

Gray: He'll figure it out.

Hamish: You're a cagey bastard. If I didn't have a healthy respect for your ability to kill me, I'd have a few more words about you quitting via text message.

Gray: Tell your more sensible half to call me.

Hamish: You think Aki is more sensible than me in the morning? Not before coffee.

In the end, it wasn't Akash who contacted him. Instead,

Caddock Stanford, one of the five rugby players who owned the Sin Bin, reached out to him to inform him they'd bought the warehouse space connected to their nightclub and intended to turn it into a restaurant. Their hunt for a head chef had thus far proven to be unsuccessful.

Gray translated that to mean that Scottie Monk, the club manager and co-owner, had chased off all the chefs. He might find the retired rugby player intriguing, but he wasn't blind to the man's terrible attitude. Why his friends had allowed Scottie to run the club still perplexed Gray.

If Gray were truly interested, Caddock suggested, then they could all get together to discuss the matter. The other co-owners, Remi Chardin, BC Brooks, and Taine Afoa would all be in Cardiff at the beginning of March. It gave him two months to make his decision.

One positive aspect of working with the former rugby players was that Gray would be able to focus completely on cooking while they hired someone else to deal with everything else. He wondered how Scottie would handle being in such close proximity to him. The man had gone out of his way to avoid him ever since they'd somehow ended up spending Christmas together.

After pouring himself another mug of coffee, Gray headed over to the laptop set up at the kitchen table. He'd make the most of those two months to think things over. *Always take advantage of opportunities when they show up, you never know when it's going to be your last chance.* Old Sam would've told him to jump at the offer.

I don't jump.

Might slowly make my way towards it, though.

CHAPTER TWO

GRAY

By the time March rolled around, Gray had come to the conclusion that running the kitchen would suit him perfectly. He'd used his two months to test recipes, create menus, and work with a few local chefs. Akash had called in a few favours with friends who gracefully allowed him into their restaurants.

Someone, likely the twins, had informed Akash about his interlude with Scottie over the holidays. The baker had, in turn, told everyone he knew. As a result, Gray's involvement with the Sin Bin's new restaurant had been kept a secret to ensure maximum amusement for all of them when Scottie found out.

As BC put it, Scottie would likely "shit a brick" when he realised who the new chef would be. Gray didn't know whether to look forward to it or to wear a Kevlar vest for protection. They were meeting up later today to finalise the details.

Caddock: Scottie's been told we're meeting up with the chef today. Meet us at noon for a tasting of your menu?

Gray: About to head out. Keep your boy out of the restaurant side. Wouldn't want to ruin the surprise.

Caddock: Sadist.

Gray: Yes. And?

Caddock: He's going to have our balls for doing this to him, unless he's too hungover to be bothered.

Gray: I'm sure he will.

Caddock: Not entirely certain you mean it the same way I meant it.

Stepping into the finished restaurant, Gray was stunned by the transformation in the former empty warehouse space. They'd brought in Caddock's husband, Francis, from Looe, who worked as an interior decorator. He'd outdone himself.

It felt like stepping into an underground prohibition-era men's club. All the booths and chairs were aged burgundy leather with antique wooden tables to match. The walls were covered in a realistic brick façade while the floors were dark mahogany to balance against the rest of the space.

Several large chandeliers hung from the ceiling. Gray had initially thought the light fixtures would stand out too much amidst the leather and wood, but seeing them all lit up in the space, he was surprised to see how well they worked. It all went perfectly.

As with the nightclub, the restaurant décor had a balanced

mixture of rugby memorabilia and vintage artwork. Visualizing the eccentric designer's concept had been difficult. Seeing it completed, Gray found it better than anything he'd even come close to imagining.

Sitting in one of the armchairs that were interspersed with the booths to test it out, Gray wondered if Francis could find one for his home. The chairs were sinfully comfortable and smelled wonderfully leathery. He definitely had to get one of them.

Right, time to check out the kitchen.

While the overwhelming theme of the dining area was vintage, Gray's kitchen seemed almost futuristic with all the state-of-the-art equipment. Standing in what might become his creative culinary space, he wondered if this might be more than he could handle. Loving to cook didn't always translate to a successful head chef.

It was a risk for all of them.

With four of the five owners, Gray had discussed at length via email how to manage things. The restaurant, Ruck, would be exclusive small parties, reservation only. He would control the menu each night, offering a fresh experience five nights a week.

It was a novel concept he thought would provide him plenty of room to explore his culinary talents. The risk came from not knowing if anyone in Cardiff would buy into it.

He didn't believe in failure; it would succeed.

It has to.

Wanting to impress his new backers, Gray got to work preparing a truly impressive spread with boeuf bourguignon toast, prime rib sliders, and whisky-glazed wings for starters, and a brown butter roast chicken with smashed potatoes for the entrée. Akash had brought over a selection of cakes; he'd be providing desserts for the restaurant for the foreseeable future. There were also potential future menus on paper to show the owners.

Fuck me.

This felt like more work than boot camp—it isn't, but it sure as fuck feels like it.

"Oi. Gray? You in here?" Caddock barged into the kitchen. "We're all seated out there. Scottie's late—as ever. You ready to feed the ravenous horde?"

"You've got to stop reading Francis's novels. Scottie's only late because he decided to try to drink us all under the table again. He's probably still sleeping it off." BC strode in behind his friend. They both started towards the platters lined across one of the counters, only to freeze in place when Gray scowled at them. "Bugger. You ever consider refereeing? You've got the 'punish the naughty rugby boys' look down perfectly."

Punish the naughty boys?

They've no fucking clue.

If they only knew….

Deciding not to go for the easy joke, Gray closed the two former rugby players out of his kitchen. He didn't want them to get an early sampling of the food. His reputation preceded him, and they went without an argument.

When the server borrowed from the nightclub arrived to help him, Gray managed to get all the starters plated up without any trouble. He followed the waiter out into the restaurant to find the five rugby players waiting, seated around one of the larger tables. A slightly bleary-eyed Scottie took one look at him, muttered a few creative curses, smacked a laughing Caddock on the head, and bolted from the dining room.

"Well, he handled that as brilliantly as expected," Remi, the lone Frenchman amongst the group of friends, remarked caustically. "Should someone retrieve him? I'm not in the mood to cater to the Monk temper today."

"Bloody Frenchie," BC muttered. "I am not sodding it."

"Me either," Caddock chimed in readily.

Gray exchanged a knowing look with Taine, who was the only serious one amongst the five, perhaps outside of Remi. "I'll hunt the rabbit."

"He's sodding terrifying," BC whispered to Caddock, eyes darting toward their new chef. Gray chuckled darkly. "Are we sure he wasn't an assassin?"

"Just a marine."

"They're never *just* marines." Remi met Gray's stony gaze without flinching. "I doubt assassin is the right word for a decorated marine sniper and sergeant major."

Interesting.

It sounded as if Remi had done a bit of research on him. *Background check, maybe?* It wouldn't have been all that difficult to find a bit about his service history. The vast majority of his deployments before and after becoming a drill instructor were likely declassified.

With a nod to Remi, Gray made his way out of the restaurant. He blinked in the rare spring sunlight. His eyes quickly adjusted to allow him to spot Scottie, leaning against a nearby wall and muttering to himself.

"You've been avoiding me." Gray walked purposefully forward until the toes of his shoes almost touched the edge of Scottie's trainers. "Did I scare you?"

"Hardly." Scottie tilted his head to scowl at him. "Fuck off. My head's still killing me."

"What do they call you rugby boys? Lions? Is that it? You're no fucking lion. You're a kitten who's barely off his mother's milk." Gray easily dodged the clumsy punch thrown his direction. Even without his thirty-plus years of military experience, avoiding the swing of a drunken man required little effort. "C'mon, kitten. Didn't your mom tell you not to roll around in the dirt?"

"She called me her little fucking bastard and told me to drink bleach." Scottie jerked his shoulders up in a hard shrug. "Didn't learn much from the twat or anyone else in my family, come to think of it."

"So? Want a medal?" Gray used his forearm to pin Scottie to the brick wall behind him. "Want a fucking trophy for surviving? Guess what? They don't hand them out. I should know. I'd be first in line to receive one. You don't get a pass from common courtesy because life hasn't been fair. You're not the only human being to survive a childhood of abuse and pain. Get the fuck over yourself."

"I'm not a fucking kitten." Scottie tried to shove him away, but Gray held him still. "What the fuck do you want?"

"Well, you're certainly not a lion." Gray bent forward to drag his nose along the side of Scottie's neck, biting him just above his collar. "No, not a lion. You also still reek of booze. Forget to shower this morning?"

"Fuck you."

Gray couldn't resist a smirk when the evidence of Scottie's arousal pressed against his leg. "Get back inside for the tasting, kitten. We'll finish this later."

Striding away from the heavily breathing man without a second look, Gray reached down to subtly adjust his dick. *Fuck.* Scottie brought out the best and worst in him. Taking things slowly wasn't proving to be easy by any stretch of the imagination.

Maybe I'll pay him a visit tonight.

Tuck him into bed like a good boy.

CHAPTER THREE

SCOTTIE

When will this end?

If there's a god out there, please fucking end this madness before I lose it.

When Taine had texted him about meeting at Ruck, Scottie barely managed to dress himself and make it safely to the restaurant. He'd seen the worried and, in some cases, judgemental looks his friends sent his way. It was fairly obvious he'd overdone it with alcohol. *Again.*

The food tasting meant Scottie had to sit through two hours of what seemed like pure torture. He had no doubt Gray went out of his way to brush against him; even just the smell of the man made his shaft hard. *Fucking wanker. Fuck. I could use a wank.* His mood plummeted further into hell when Caddock strong-armed him into helping the chef in the kitchen.

"You were late. Make yourself useful." Caddock nudged him in the side to encourage him to get up out of his chair. "Are you scared? Is Scottie intimidated by the big bad American?"

"Go fuck yourself with a fork." Scottie threw his napkin into his friend's face. Why didn't they understand he wanted to be home, sleeping off yet another hangover in peace? "He'll manage on his own. He doesn't need me holding his sodding hand. And you can all stop throwing those looks at me—*wankers*."

"Scott." Remi drew his attention with the hard edge to his voice. The Frenchie usually disapproved of his behaviour, but he'd never sounded quite so terse. "You're the manager and a co-owner of the Sin Bin and by extension this restaurant. If you can't act like a sober adult, perhaps you shouldn't be in charge of the day-to-day operations."

"You—" Scottie shot to his feet, and only a quick reach from Taine saved his chair from being knocked to the floor. He met the steely gaze of Remi for a full minute before deciding the battle wasn't worth fighting. "Fine. I'll go see if the old fucker needs any help. And I am sober—just hungover."

Fuckwits.

Making his way through the dining room, Scottie found the chef putting the last touches on all the desserts. Most had been done in collaboration with Akash, but the pots de crème had been made by Gray. The entire kitchen smelled strongly of rich, bitter chocolate and sweet caramel.

"Want a taste?" Gray held up one of the square dishes holding the silky dessert. "C'mere."

Scottie had no idea why his legs took him across the room until he stood within arm's reach of the smug American, who always managed to make questions sound like demands. "What?"

Cocky wanker.

Fuck.

Stop thinking about his cock and wanking.

Fuck me.

No, that's not helpful either.

"Closer." Gray waved the chocolate pudding in his hand while grabbing a spoon from the nearby counter. "Ask nicely."

"Give me the fucking chocolate," he snapped.

No one had ever accused Scottie of being a nice man.

Ever.

Particularly after a long night out.

His angry scowl did nothing to deter Gray who appeared amused by it. *I'm not playing his fucking game even if he does keep my cock in a constant and almost painful state of interest. I don't want GI Joe. I want someone like Akash. So why the hell am I so hard when I'm around him?*

"If you're not interested in what I can offer, the door is behind you. I'm certain you can exit as easily as you entered." Gray dipped a spoon into the chocolate and offered it to him. "If, however, you want to explore the depth of lust that's had your dick at attention since I called you, kitten, you'll ask nicely."

"Fuck—"

"Me. I'm aware." Gray cut him off before Scottie could finish. "Out the door or ask nicely?"

"Neither. I'm only here to see if you need help with

anything." Scottie gritted his teeth to keep from saying anything else. He wouldn't cave to Gray or to his own desires. *Not yet. Not until I fucking understand them, or maybe after a few pints or seven.* "Want a hand or not?"

Gray licked the chocolate from the spoon while his brown eyes stayed on Scottie, who felt a little fainter than he wanted to admit. "Sure you don't want to ask nicely?"

Despite the interest from the lower half of his body, Scottie spun on his heel and slammed through the double doors leading out of the kitchen. He ignored the calls from his friends. For the sake of his sanity, he desperately needed out of the building.

Grabbing his helmet off the handlebars of his Triumph, Scottie swung his leg over and got seated. He'd left his jacket inside, but the cold ride might do him as much good as an icy shower. His thoughts faded away as he pulled out of the parking lot.

He rode.

And rode until he found himself sitting outside of Gray's home.

Why the fuck am I still letting him get to me?

He knew why. Gray had gotten under his skin with the sudden and surprisingly intoxicating idea of submission. The idea of surrendering control was something he'd been unable to get out of his mind since Christmas.

Fucking idiotic.

I'm not doing it.

I could text him.

Scottie: You up? We should talk about the restaurant

opening next week.

Gray: At one in the morning?

Scottie: I'm outside your place.

Gray: I'm aware. It only took thirty minutes for you to work up the courage to text me, kitten.

Scottie: Do you want to fucking talk or not?

Gray: Door's been open for the last fifteen minutes. I'm just waiting for you to decide to come inside. Fire is lit, got two glasses of scotch, and a cigar. Get your ass in out of the cold.

This is moronic.

What am I doing? Why do I want to see where the hell he's going to take me? I'm not that hard up for a good fuck.

I'm so bloody screwed.

CHAPTER FOUR

GRAY

When the rumble of an old bike brought him out of his doze by the fire in the living room, Gray immediately knew Scottie had come for a visit. As the minutes went by, his amusement grew at the obvious struggle going on in the man's mind. He'd always enjoyed the mental aspects of dominance as well as the physical, so the agony of Scottie fighting through his decision to submit thrilled him.

Comfortable in the chair Francis had helped him pilfer from the restaurant, Gray lounged lazily in nothing but a pair of low-rise briefs, suddenly happy to have decided not to get fully dressed after his earlier shower. *Scottie's reaction to me in nothing but my skivvies will certainly prove entertaining.*

Gray picked up his cigar again to take a quick puff before

reaching for his glass of scotch just as his front door opened. *Fuck. I've turned myself into a porn cliché.*

"Hey? Old man." Scottie slammed the door shut and rounded the corner, only to come to an immediate stop in the centre of the room. His gaze drifted over Gray's seated form. *"Fuck."*

Gray set his glass aside and grabbed his Zippo to relight his cigar. He pointed toward the sofa directly across from him. "Sit before your legs give out on you."

Foreplay certainly had its place, but Gray thought they both knew Scottie hadn't ridden through the bitterly cold spring weather to talk about menus. He puffed lazily on his cigar and waited. The next move had to come from the former rugby player.

With a ridiculous amount of out of character stammering, Scottie delivered his excuse for showing up uninvited. He wanted to go over the schedule for the restaurant, which was due to open the last week of March. They stared at each other in silence until Gray finally snuffed out his cigar.

Let's see how far he's ready to push himself.

Gray slowly rose to his feet and casually crossed the distance between them until he loomed over the seated Scottie. "Why are you here, kitten? No horseshit. Tell me the truth."

Scottie's eyes remained laser-focused on the underwear-covered cock in front of him. "I don't fucking know."

"Not good enough," Gray stated sternly. He wanted there to be a clear understanding between them—even while he enjoyed the unconscious way Scottie's tongue continually ran across his lips. "We're going to be crystal clear about this from the start. Aren't we?"

"Yes." He cleared his throat twice before he got the single word out.

"Yes? Yes, what?" Gray moved one step closer, his shaft pulsing in anticipation of everything he'd fantasised about within his grasp. "I believe 'yes, sir' has a nice ring to it. Don't you agree, kitten?"

"I…." Scottie trailed off and clenched his jaw tightly with his eyes never drifting away from the bulge inches from his face. "Yes, sir."

"Felt good, didn't it?" Gray dropped his hand firmly on Scottie's closely shaved head, pushing him face first into his groin. "You enjoyed the little jolt to your dick when you gave in. It's the greatest high in the world. We'll go slow, at first. You want me to stop—you say 'halt.' You want me to slow down—it's 'check fire.' If we're good to go, it's 'as you were.' Do you understand?"

"Yes." Scottie jolted forward when Gray cuffed him lightly on the back of the head. "Yes, sir."

"Good." Gray wanted to have a far more detailed conversation about their individual expectations, but it would be better without the haze of lust. They both needed to think clearly about it. "*Good.* I'm going to be in control. No fucking doubt about it. You don't touch yourself or me unless I tell you. We'll go deeper another day. But for now, are we good to go?"

Scottie nodded.

"Be a good kitten and use your words," Gray smirked at the flash of anger and desire that quickly went across

Scottie's face.

"Yes, sir."

Hard dicks don't help with clear thinking.

Using his hand on Scottie's head, Gray guided him off the couch and onto his knees. He pressed Scottie's face further against his shaft, grinning when he began to suck on it through the fabric. His lips and tongue worked over the heavy bulge, leaving damp spots in their wake.

"Good boy." Gray had waited patiently for months to get Scottie on his knees, and he intended to enjoy every single moment of it. "Take them off."

"What?"

"Your mouth only serves one purpose right now—and that's not fucking talking. Take off my briefs." Gray smacked the hand that reached up toward him. "Use your teeth."

Though clearly bristling under the command, Scottie caught the waistband of his briefs and dragged them down with his teeth. Gray kicked them coolly to the side before crooking his finger to draw Scottie's attention to his now freed erection. He wanted to experience those lips on him without the barrier of fabric between them.

He's going to have to grow his hair out—I do love having something to yank a boy around by.

With his hand cupping the back of Scottie's head, Gray slapped his hard cock against dry, parted lips. Scottie flicked his tongue out reflexively for a taste. The teasing game of denying both of them what they wanted lasted for several minutes.

"Open up." Gray lost his patience with playing around.

He thrust shallowly into the waiting mouth, though he issued a warning when Scottie's hand came to rest on his thigh. "No touching, be good. I'd enjoy punishing you as much as rewarding you."

The fire in Scottie's eyes never really died down. Gray soaked it all in while splitting his attention between driving between those surprisingly supple lips and nudging his kitten's cock with his toes. They were both definitely deriving the same amount of pleasure from their first time together.

Gray lightly kicked Scottie's hand away when he reached down to unzip his own trousers to stroke himself. "What the fuck did I say about your hands?"

Dragging the head of his cock around already swollen lips, Gray enjoyed the almost dazed gleam in the eyes of the man at his feet. Scottie licked whatever part of his shaft he could reach. *Damn. This is better than I imagined it would be. Oh, the places I can take him.*

Oh, the places I can fuck him.

With his hands on either side of his new sub's head, Gray once again tossed teasing to the side. He hammered into the willing warmth of Scottie's mouth. Time would tell how well suited to his new role he actually was.

"Are you humping my foot, kitten? Can't help yourself, can you?" Gray enjoyed the physical demonstration of how deep this could go. "Good boy."

Pulling out after several hard thrusts, Gray stroked himself through the final moments of climax while Scottie nuzzled at his balls. He covered his upturned face. The evidence of his pleasure dripped across Scottie's cheek and forehead.

"You want to get off? Want to come?" Gray teased him cruelly, rubbing his bare foot against Scottie's jeans-covered shaft. "Use my leg."

"Wha—" Scottie was cut off by Gray pushing his toes into his groin again. He moaned when the foot pressed even harder. "*Fuck.*"

"Keep going. Such a good boy." Gray continued to taunt Scottie, who began to practically hump his leg. "Let's get more comfortable. Shall we?"

Returning to his leather chair, Gray sank into it and told Scottie to crawl over to him. It wasn't long before he frotted against his stretched-out leg. *I can't fucking wait to see him naked, stretched out in front of me. I'll break him into a thousand pieces and see how easily he comes back together for me.*

"I've got—"

"Good kitten. Go on, then." Gray smirked when Scottie went to undo his jeans. "You're going to make a mess of your underwear for me. And you won't be wearing them again."

"Fuck. I can't."

"Yes, you can. And what did I say about speaking?" Gray's fingers easily found Scottie's nipples through his T-shirt, twisting first one then the other. He wasn't surprised when the man almost immediately bucked against his leg. "Pleasure and pain. I'm going to teach you so much about treading the fine line between."

Once Scottie stopped panting and collapsed against his legs, Gray decided a quick wash might be a good idea. He'd made sure his home contained a standing shower large enough for two men. It was time for another test.

How many aspects will he enjoy?

Being ordered to wash first Gray and then himself didn't seem to faze Scottie at all. He was clumsy, and his jaw clenched throughout it as if he mentally struggled with himself, but his cock hardened and stayed that way. *Submission is a beautiful thing.*

They collapsed into bed after Scottie finished cleaning and drying them both. Gray drifted off to sleep with the full expectation of finding the bed empty when he woke up. He was surprised to find Scottie still snoring beside him when his alarm went off at seven.

Fuck.

I can't wait to have him again.

CHAPTER FIVE

SCOTTIE

What the fuck did I do?

Waking up without a hangover or still drunk had been a nice change. Scottie thought a stiff drink might help him make sense of everything. He certainly found it hard to wrap his mind around how much he'd enjoyed the release of submitting to Gray.

All the whirling, chaotic rage in his mind had calmed for the briefest of moments. Scottie had only ever felt a similar freedom on the rugby pitch. He hated how much he craved it again.

Both the rugby and the submission.

Scottie rolled over on his back and stretched his arms out in the empty bed. He rarely spent the night with his sexual partners and usually ducked out in the early morning hours when he did. The smell of breakfast forced him to drag himself up out of the covers.

Right.

Clothes.

A glance around the room told him someone had clearly made off with his jeans and T-shirt. *I'm not running around with my bits out. I've been vulnerable enough for one day.* Scottie yawned loudly and cleared the sleep from his eyes with a rough swipe of his hand.

It was impossible to deny he'd thoroughly enjoyed last night. Only in the light of day, he didn't know how to process all of it. Time alone to think would be his next priority.

After I find my fucking clothes.

Following the smell of coffee and sausage, Scottie found the former marine standing in front of the hob in his briefs and an old USMC T-shirt. He watched Gray for several minutes while he moved confidently around the kitchen. The man had definite passion when it came to cooking.

"I'm fucking starved." Scottie noticed his jeans and T-shirt folded on one of the stools that surrounded the island in the centre of the kitchen. "Where are my boxers?"

"You can manage without them." Gray nodded toward the fridge across from him. "Juice? Milk? Or something more caffeinated?"

"I can manage without them?" Scottie found himself ogling at a turned back as Gray completely ignored his dumbfounded question. *Wanker.* He dragged the freshly washed T-shirt over his head, pulled on his jeans, and wandered barefoot over to grab the mug of coffee on the counter. "Am I supposed to not have socks either?"

"They're by the door in your shoes." Gray smacked his hand with the wooden spatula in his hand. "Never fuck with a marine's coffee, kitten. Pour your own damn mug."

Before Scottie could stop himself, he'd wrested the spatula out of Gray's loose grip and snapped it in half. They both stared at the broken utensil for a few seconds. *Right. Fuck. Maybe I should've paid attention in all those anger management classes.* He flung the pieces in his hand to the floor and fled the room.

Fumbling with his socks and then his riding boots, Scottie managed to get them on before a fully dressed Gray strode toward him. He had no desire to discuss anything with the man. His helmet and leather jacket lay by the door, and he made a quick escape.

Well, you're a fucking cowardly twat.

His stomach grumbled over the missed breakfast. Scottie grew more disgusted with himself during the ride across Cardiff. The icy rain battering him kept him focused on the road and not his internal angst.

"Scottie?"

He jerked out of his daze to find a concerned Remi standing beside him on the kerb. "Thought you'd gone back to your Cornish ginger."

"You know my wife's name." Remi scowled at him. "You've sat here for almost twenty minutes in the rain. Are you hoping to turn hypothermic?"

"Fuck off." Scottie slowly got off his bike and shook his

arms out a bit. They'd started to cramp up on him from the damp cold and his fists being so tightly clenched. "Did I forget a meeting?"

"Francis is here making the changes to décor that we asked for." Remi stepped into his path when Scottie started toward the club. "Why don't we grab coffee across the street?"

"Is Caddock still hacked off about what I said to little Frannie?"

"Don't be an arsehole, Scott." Remi waited until Scottie had removed his helmet and placed it on the handlebar before he grabbed his arm to force him toward the café. "Francis hasn't done anything to deserve your nonsense. We'll have breakfast, and you can tell me why you're as pale as a ghost."

His initial thought was to argue, but Remi's glare changed his mind. Of all his friends, the Frenchie intimidated him when none of the others even fazed him. He wouldn't cross the man for anything, not without copious amounts of liquor involved.

They squashed uncomfortably around the only available two-seater table at the café. Remi stuck with a plain coffee while Scottie ordered two bacon sarnies to go with his hot drink. He dumped enough sugar to rot his teeth into his mug for something to do to avoid the steady stare from the man across from him.

Scottie eventually lost his patience with his friend. "What? Why the sodding hell are you glaring at me?"

"You've got the most fantastic love bite that I've ever seen on the side of your jaw." He chuckled when Scottie snarled at him. "I'll leave the jokes for BC. What happened last night to cause you to be so out of sorts?"

"Nothing."

"I haven't seen you so pale since the time you broke three ribs during a qualifier." Remi held his mug in both hands, clearly enjoying the warmth. "You know, friends of mine have seen your American at a few of the Cardiff munches in the past."

Scottie inhaled coffee into his mouth and coughed violently as a result. "Wanker."

"I've never seen him—but Sarah and I attend ones closer to home usually." He dropped the insight into his personal life rather casually, to Scottie's surprise. The Frenchman tended to closely guard his relationship with his wife. "You share this information, Scott, and I will break your nose—*again*."

Arsehole.

"Why tell me, then?" Scottie asked after the server had dropped off his sandwiches.

Remi stole a handful of the chips on Scottie's plate before answering. "You won't talk to your American about your fears. Who else do you know that plays in the fetish pool aside from me?"

"I've got twenty quid on Tens." Scottie had watched the man with his boyfriend and wondered about their relationship a few times. He blinked in surprise when a chip hit him between the eyes. "What?"

"You leave Freddie and Taine alone." Remi stabbed a chip in his direction for emphasis. "They've had enough troubles without you being your usual self."

Scottie gave a shrug and pulled his plate out of his friend's reach when he went for another handful of chips. "Order your own, you thieving bastard."

"Stingy." Remi signalled one of the servers to place an order and took the chance to ask for a top-up of their coffees. "Has Gray discussed what specific flavour of relationship he wants?"

"Remi." Scottie managed not to shout at his friend. "No, no, no, no, no. I'm not fucking chatting with you about this."

"Was it your first scene?"

"I will break *your* nose and send you back to your wife bleeding," Scottie ground out angrily.

"You would try and fail—like last time." Remi paused when the server brought over his order of chips and topped up their coffee. "Let me guess what happened. You enjoyed submitting. You woke up, panicked that you found pleasure in it, and ran off."

"I don't know." Scottie took a large bite of one of his sandwiches and chewed slowly while glaring across the table. "And I don't see how it's any of your fucking business."

"So, yes." He pointed one of his chips at Scottie for a second time. "Why didn't you stay and talk to him about your fears?"

"I wasn't fucking afraid." Scottie's voice sounded weak even to himself. He chugged down the coffee, ignoring the slight burn of the hot liquid. "I'm done."

Throwing money on the table to cover his part of the bill, Scottie grabbed the remaining half of the sandwich and stormed out of the café. He'd been pushed enough for one day. Remi didn't immediately follow him, allowing him to make it up to his office without being harassed by anyone else.

What bothered him most was Remi hadn't been wrong; Scottie just didn't have it in him to answer them yet. He had enjoyed it and panicked as a result. Gray had been everything Scottie hadn't known he needed.

And I fucking ran like a coward.

Shit.

What am I doing?

Best sex I've ever had. Best night of sleep I've had in ages. And I ruin it by sneaking out?

The act of submission had freed Scottie in ways he hadn't imagined possible. He'd surrendered completely to it. He wanted the feeling again—over and over, which terrified him and made him never want it again. *Fuck.*

Scottie collapsed into his desk chair, setting his sandwich on top of a stack of paper and dropping his head back with a grown. *Wonder if anyone would notice if I drowned myself in an ocean of whisky.* "I will not turn into my sodding father. I fucking won't."

One drink can't hurt, though.

The first shot of whisky burned all the way down, the third dulled the pain, and the seventh numbed him to everything going on around him. Slumped in his chair in his office, Scottie drank his way through one of the most expensive bottles the Sin Bin served. He stayed behind the locked door the entire day in a stupor, feeling wretched and so much like his father that reaching for another drink seemed the only answer.

"Scottie?"

A heavy banging jerked Scottie out of his sleep.

He immediately grunted in pain when his head connected with the unforgiving wood of the underside of his desk. *Why the hell am I on the floor in the first place?* Carefully extracting himself out from underneath it, he swayed on his feet for a moment and clutched at his chair to avoid slumping to the ground.

"Scottie. I know you're in there; I'll bash this bloody door in if you don't open it." Taine jiggled the handle roughly a few times, as if trying to make a point. "You're not dead, are you?"

Wanker.

With a pounding head and blurry vision, Scottie managed to make it across the room to unlock the door. Taine crossed his arms and glared at him. He waited for his old rugby mate to lecture him. *Fuck. Time hasn't changed anything, I'm still being told off for acting like a stupid arse.*

Taine opened his mouth and then appeared to reconsider barely a second later. He shook his head slowly. "All right, lad, why don't I take you home? We can manage the club for a night without you."

"I'll be brilliant after a few coffees," Scottie argued with a confidence he didn't actually feel; even the thought of caffeine made his stomach churn. *How much did I actually drink?* "What time is it?"

"Five."

"In the afternoon?" Scottie glanced around in confusion at the lack of staff. "Where is everyone? We'll be opening soon."

"Five in the morning, you absolutely idiotic knobdobber." Taine's slight Scottish brogue always seemed more pronounced when he swore. Part Maori and part Scot, the massive retired rugby player looked more the former and sounded more the latter. "You've either drunk or slept through an entire day."

"Fuck." Scottie drew the word out slowly. He gripped the frame of the door. "*Fuck*."

Taine's scowl faded into something more like concern. "Do you want to talk about it?"

"No."

"Thank God." Taine rested a hand on Scottie's shoulder and used it to ease him out of the office. "We're worried about you."

"We?"

"Look, you're an arse, but you're still our friend. We've known each other for ages." Taine carefully led him down the flights of stairs to get to the first-floor exit. "Whatever you might think, we're not letting you drink yourself into an early grave. You hear me?"

"Don't be so fucking dramatic," Scottie scoffed at him. He didn't want to consider the truth behind his friend's concern. The Monk family had a history of alcohol-related deaths; an ignominious distinction in which he obviously partook. "I'm fine."

"You're not." Taine pushed him out into the crisp night air. "Why don't I get you a takeaway for later?"

Thinking about food made Scottie queasy enough to have to pause to take a few deep breaths before he was sick. Taine chuckled beside him. *Fucking bastard.* They eventually made it to his friend's SUV, and he tumbled into the passenger seat, fumbling with the seat belt before getting situated.

"Scottie?"

He shook his head to clear it, only to realise that he'd fallen asleep. "Where are we?"

"The hospital."

Scottie sat up slowly and glanced around to find the scenery had changed quite significantly. "Why the fuck am I in a hospital bed?"

Taine placed a hand on his shoulder to keep him seated. "You passed out. I couldn't wake you up. How much did you drink?"

Scottie ran his fingers vigorously across his head. "Not a clue. It's all a blur. I honestly can't remember. What happened?"

"You almost drank yourself into the grave," Taine remarked bluntly.

"You're lucky you didn't need a catheter or to be intubated. The doctor decided the IV drip was sufficient." Freddie stepped up beside Taine and leaned into him when he wrapped an arm around his shoulders. "Have you heard of alcohol poisoning?"

Scottie shrugged and glared down at the tube stuck into his arm. He couldn't help twitching at the thought of a catheter. How much had he drunk? The last clear memory was having breakfast with Remi—and trying to avoid a conversation about Gray.

"You could've died from a heart attack, from seizures, or even from choking on your own vomit." Freddie brutally went through each possible danger of alcohol poisoning without giving him a chance to process. "I've seen cases where individuals inhaled their own bile and the damage to their lungs was fatal."

"I get it. *Fuck.*" Scottie rubbed his chest absently at the sudden tightness he felt just considering what might've happened. "Aren't nurses supposed to offer comfort?"

"I would, but you're too stubborn for it to help." Freddie led Taine across the room, where they had a brief whispered conversation. "I'll see if I can find the doctor."

Taine returned to the chair near Scottie's bed. "They're going to suggest you either enter rehab or perhaps Alcoholics Anonymous."

"Not a fucking chance," Scottie snarled instinctively at the idea. "I can manage on my own."

"You could've died in my vehicle, and I would've had no idea how to help you." He slammed his fist against the mattress, jolting Scottie slightly. "You either get some help, or you're done as the manager of the Sin Bin. None of us wants to stand over your grave because you couldn't be arsed to try to defeat your family demons."

"Tens."

Taine held his hand up to stop Scottie. "Think about it. They're keeping you for a few more hours at least. Not watching my friend die. Understand?"

"Wanker." Scottie couldn't manage to inflect any true bite to the word. "I'll think about it."

The obvious concern beneath Taine's well-meant bullying forced Scottie to really consider what he'd said. Did he want to turn into his father? *And grandfather, and aunt, and uncle, and mother, and just about everyone else in my fucking family. Can I do this?*

"Scott?"

"Hmm?" He glanced away from the IV drip to find Taine still watching him. "What?"

"You're not alone. You know that, right? You might be an annoying as shite knobdobber, but you're our little brother. You're family. We don't abandon family." Taine grabbed his hand firmly, not letting go when Scottie tried to tug it away. "You'll get through this battle just like you did on the rugby pitch."

CHAPTER SIX

GRAY

"Did you hear about Monk?" Nye asked, joining him in the company gym that they'd been gracious enough to allow Gray to continue to use even after he'd left to pursue cooking. "He's in the hospital, or he was."

Gray paused in the middle of a deadlift to send a warning glare toward the former British Marine who worked with Hamish and Wyatt. "What's that phrase you use all the time? Piss off."

"Uncultured swine," Nye teased. "I'm not trying to make anything of it. Shanti told me about your interest in him, and I thought you'd want to know."

With a grunt of acknowledgement, Gray returned his attention to his workout in the hopes of ending the conversation. He'd received several texts early in the morning about Scottie's emergency room visit. His first instinct was to go the hospital immediately, but he'd decided that waiting would be a wiser decision.

If Scottie had truly decided to deal with his binge drinking, then Gray would only serve as an unwanted distraction. He'd check in on him in a few days.

His mind was set, and he had no intentions of wavering—until a few days later his phone buzzed.

Scottie: Where the fuck have you been?

Gray: At the restaurant?

Scottie: Not what I meant.

Gray: I figured you'd need some time to figure things out for yourself.

Scottie: No one fucking thinks I can figure things out for myself. Isn't that the point of all of this?

Scottie: You busy?

Gray: Prepping for tonight's service. Why?

Scottie: I'm not allowed at the Sin Bin for a month.

Gray: What are you doing with yourself?

Scottie: Freddie set me up with some volunteer shit. Supposed to be helping someone who was struck by a drunk driver.

Gray: Shock aversion therapy. Showing you the potential long-term consequences of being a drunken fuckstick.

Scottie: Is this your idea of being supportive? You're fucking shit at it.

Gray: You want honesty, text me. You want bullshit answers that make you feel better? You're purring at the

wrong tree, kitten.

Scottie: Fuck off.

Gray: You texted me.

After a twenty-minute silence, Gray assumed the conversation had ended. He returned his attention to the sampling of the menu. Each day he cooked up a single serving of whatever they'd be giving to customers; he wanted the staff to taste all of it and be able to speak with confidence to customers.

While the diners might not get to choose their courses, it worked best when they knew in detail what to expect from the evening. Initial reviews for Ruck had all been overwhelmingly positive. He could admit to himself having a lifelong dream at his fingertips was surreal.

The servers joined him around noon to begin setting up for the afternoon and evening. They demolished the plates that he set out for them, exclaiming in particular over his new exploration with bite-sized beef Wellingtons. He planned on doing an entire series for miniature versions of the tired old standard; having complete control over a menu meant freedom to experiment.

Scottie: I'm having coffee across the street from Ruck.

Gray: Is that an invitation?

Scottie: No.

Gray: I'll be over shortly.

After finishing up his meeting with the servers, Gray made his way over to the café only to find Scottie sitting outside on the kerb with two Styrofoam cups in hand. He offered one up when Gray sat beside him. He appeared tired and worn while staring into his coffee.

"Predicting the future? You'll need tea leaves, not coffee grounds." Gray found it hard not to smirk when he sipped his own drink and discovered Scottie had managed to order it perfectly. "What do you need, kitten? You didn't text me for a warm and fuzzy cuddle. Neither of us is the type."

"Fuck off." Scottie scowled at him. "And I'm not a kitten."

Gray went to stand up only for the man beside him to grab his arm and drag him back down. "Yes?"

"I almost died."

Gray watched Scottie out of the corner of his eyes, not wanting to spook the surprisingly vulnerable-sounding man, whose fingers trembled slightly around his cup. "Alcohol poisoning will do that to a person. You sure you don't want to try rehab?"

"Tens suggested Castle Craig in Scotland." Scottie shrugged indifferently. "Don't see how it can help more than the A-fucking-A shit. What do you think?"

"I think you don't give a fuck what anyone else thinks. I also know you have to make the decision on your own and do it for yourself, or it won't change anything." Gray chugged down his cooled coffee and ached for the angry man at his side. He knew with a painful familiarity the rage that came from a childhood of abuse and pain, but he also had experience with pulling out of the trap of history repeating itself. "The question is, Scott, do you want to be your father? Do you want to be another statistic in your family?"

"I'm not drunk every fucking night."

"Maybe not." Gray honestly believed the real problem

lay with Scottie's anger—deal with it, and his tendency to occasionally drink himself into a dangerous stupor would likely go away. "I'm not a professional. Perhaps you should ask one before you wind up needing more than a couple of nights at the hospital."

"Maybe." Scottie went back to staring blindly into his coffee as if it held all the answers for him. "I don't drink every fucking night."

"Yes, and repeating yourself like a petulant toddler isn't going to make your case to anyone—myself included." Gray easily blocked the elbow sent his direction. "Here's what I would do in your place, kitten. I'd speak to the people at Castle Craig. Go for a visit. What do you have to lose?"

"I'm not a fucking kitten." Scottie turned his head away to glance down the street.

"When you act like the lion you claim to be, I might reconsider." Gray leaned forward until his lips hovered against Scottie's neck. His breath wafted across the sensitive skin, and he couldn't help smirking at the way Scottie shuddered pleasurably at the sensation. "If you want me to stop calling you kitten, perhaps you should say it, instead of insisting you aren't one."

"Fucking wanker," Scottie grumbled into his coffee.

"That's what I thought." Gray shifted back and stretched his long legs out in front of him into the street. "Why don't you come help me in the kitchen?"

"Not allowed into the club."

"The restaurant isn't the club—and if you take a drink in front of me, I'll have to punish you." Gray winked at him before getting to his feet and reaching down to yank Scottie up as well. "Sitting around moaning at the world won't change a fucking thing."

"Wanker."

They cleaned up together. Gray suspected Scottie threw himself into the manual labour to avoid thinking about his problems. He wondered if submission had cleared Scottie's mind enough to force him to see some truths about himself.

It wouldn't be the first time.

Gray put away the last of his knives and twisted around to lean against the counter. "Want me to make the drive with you?"

"To Castle Craig?"

Gray knew the other rugby players would volunteer, but they'd likely poke at Scottie in the wrong way. "What's the harm in seeing the premises? Talking to a few of the counsellors."

"Don't need it."

"Then think of it as a vacation with a fucking detour." Gray couldn't make him go, but he'd cajole strongly. "Voodoo says you learn a lot about someone on a road trip. Think you can handle it?"

"*Fuck.*"

CHAPTER SEVEN

SCOTTIE

They took the long way to West Linton, Scotland. Three hours into the ten-hour journey, Scottie considered abandoning ship. The dare in Gray's eyes kept him in the passenger seat of the Range Rover that had been borrowed from Hamish.

The quiet companionship gave Scottie time to consider rehab. Fear and anger swirled around in him. *I don't fucking need help.* How many times had he heard those same words from various members of his family?

Shit.

When they finally drove into the visitor car park at the castle after spending the night at a hotel, fear had completely trumped anger. Scottie gripped the seat belt across his chest so tightly it dug into his palms. He didn't want to face the truth of his problems.

Gray pulled the keys out of the ignition then reached a hand out to carefully ease Scottie's hand away from the belt. "You can do this."

"What?"

"Whatever it is you find behind the castle walls to help." Gray hadn't pressed him through the long hours to get to Scotland. They'd talked about their lives, past relationships, and anything but Castle Craig. "The first steps are always the hardest, kitten."

Taking a moment to appreciate the offer of comfort, Scottie shoved the hand away from him and got out of the car. He inhaled deeply and touched a hand to the ground as he'd always done for good luck before stepping onto the rugby pitch. *I'm only here to see the facilities. They can't fucking make me do anything.*

"Mr. Monk?"

"That's me." Scottie resisted the urge to smack himself in the forehead for the pointlessness of his statement. He dragged his fingers roughly across his head. "You the tour guide?"

"Something like that. I'm part of the admissions team. If you'd follow me?"

Too late to fucking book it for the border now.

A call from Taine's adoptive father, a Scottish priest, had helped Scottie make it into the program. After initial assessments and what felt like an overload of information, they allowed Scottie to attend a group therapy session. He'd mentally written off checking into Castle Craig, convinced it wasn't for him. Listening to the pain and anguish of stories that felt so familiar they could've been his own, he stopped lying to himself.

I need help.

My drinking's out of control.

*It's affecting my business, my friends, my brother, and...
whatever the fuck this is with Gray.*

I need help.

He couldn't lie anymore about using alcohol as a way to
cope with his anger and pain. Maybe he wasn't addicted, but
his behaviour was just as self-destructive. Time would tell if
stepping outside of his life in Cardiff for a few months would
actually change anything for him.

What the fuck do I have to lose?

Nothing.

*Plenty to fucking gain if I can learn something from all this
zen shit and therapy.*

Twenty-four hours later, Scottie only slightly regretted the
decision. Gray had returned to Cardiff. And he'd started on
the "road to recovery."

He spent the first five days in detox. His personal therapist
met with him several times the first week and prepared a plan
for his three months in rehab. She wanted to focus on helping
him deal with the underlying cause of his drinking. He faced
his family demons head-on, though not always gracefully or
willingly.

*Exercise Three: Write a letter to someone expressing your
fears.*

Gray,

This is a stupid fucking exercise.

I'm afraid this place is pointless.
Scottie

Scottie,

Be a good boy, and I'll come visit you.
Gray

Scottie ignored the response for almost a week before his want to see Gray exceeded his annoyance with the man. He wrote a reply, talking over his worries about failing rehab and hurting Silus, his younger brother, in the process. Writing it out helped enough to bring him around to being more open to the process.

Still fucking hate this shit.

As the therapy continued, Scottie found himself delving deeply into childhood trauma. It hurt to remember. He'd been astounded to discover how much sharing his story, and listening to similar ones from others healed some of the old pains.

Less than two months into his stay, Gray came up to visit him for the third time. They sparred together in the boxing ring for a bit. Scottie had a hard time keeping his body from responding to the closeness.

Don't get hard in the gym at your fucking rehab.

"See you missed me." Gray, as always, missed nothing. "They told me I could have lunch with you. Why don't we clean up and grab a bite to eat?"

The quick shower allowed Scottie to get rid of his erection. *Thank fucking God.* Gray in his USMC T-shirt and tight jeans brought it back. *Damn it.* He dropped into the chair across from Gray with a frustrated groan and grabbed one of the sandwiches in front of him.

"How are you doing?" Gray asked. He held a hand up to stop Scottie from immediately offering a knee-jerk response. "Keep in mind that I actually care about you, kitten. How *are* you doing?"

Scottie found it difficult to meet the intensity in Gray's gaze. He did offer an honest answer. "Coping. Better than I've probably ever been, but it's the fucking hardest thing I've done in my life."

"Good." Gray switched over to sit directly next to Scottie, dropping a hand on his knee to squeeze firmly. "Are you proud of yourself?"

"Fu—" Scottie bit off his instinctive angry counter. He breathed out and smirked a bit sheepishly at Gray. "Not yet, but I'm getting there."

Three months in Castle Craig hadn't changed him at the core. Scottie still felt like himself. The world did seem clearer and slightly less annoying, though.

It seemed obvious now, looking back on everything, but he'd never realised how much the violence in his family truly affected him. He'd spent long weeks within various sessions all designed specifically to his issues and personality. All of the effort and time spent had helped him, but emerging from Castle Craig at the end of his three-month stint left him feeling worn out.

"Ready to head home?" Remi stood outside in the parking lot waiting for him, with Taine leaning against his Range Rover. "It's a bit of a drive so we thought we'd keep you company."

"Ten hours is more than a bit of a fucking drive." Scottie flung his bag into the back when Taine opened the rear gate. He was glad the others hadn't come along; BC and Caddock meant well, but he wasn't ready for their special brand of teasing. "Am I driving?"

"Not a chance in hell." Remi kept his keys clutched in his hand. "How many of our vehicles have you wrecked over the years?"

"Forgiveness is an important step to recovery." Scottie grinned when the Frenchie glared at him.

"Sarah sent you some of her shortbread." Remi grabbed a tin from the dashboard once they'd all piled into the vehicle, and tossed it into Scottie's lap. "Do you feel any different?"

"I don't feel like bashing your French forehead into the steering wheel. That's progress, right?" Scottie tugged on the seat belt to get a bit more room to slouch down. He worked his nail under the lid to pry it off the container to reveal a mixed batch of homemade biscuits. "Why the fuck did Sarah marry you again? Couldn't she have done better than your ugly old arse?"

Remi stretched his hand out to steal one of the cookies. "I was charming."

Taine leaned forward between the seats to grab one of the biscuits for himself. "When did you learn how to be *charming*?"

"Rugby finishing school." Remi retorted sarcastically.

While they fell into the familiar teasing of one another, Scottie breathed an internal sigh of relief. One of his greatest worries about returning to his normal life had been his friends walking on eggshells around him. The three months hadn't so much changed him as given him the right tools to deal with everything going on around and inside him.

His main therapist had counselled him to set clear boundaries for himself in relation to work at the Sin Bin. Scottie had no intentions of spiralling out-of-control again, but he had to live his life. His goal for now was to find a way to create a healthier balance in his life.

With everyone who worked with him at Castle Craig, they'd created a plan for him to put to work in Cardiff. He'd continue to see a therapist locally, once a week at first. It would hopefully keep him on track.

One of the things that had helped him greatly was getting into boxing. After his rugby career ended, Scottie hadn't found a physical outlet. Working out didn't do as much for him as a release for his emotions as being in sports had. He'd been surprised when his therapist suggested getting into the ring.

It worked, as well.

One of his goals upon returning to Cardiff was to find a boxing gym. Scottie was enjoying being clear-headed. He didn't want to lose it by throwing away all of his progress.

"Heard from Gray?" Remi drew him out of his thoughts.

"Why?" Scottie snapped defensively.

"Don't be so testy." Taine snagged another biscuit and scooted back into his seat. "Freddie said our marine chef drove up to see you a few times."

Scottie stared pointedly out at the passing countryside and ignored the sniggering coming from his two friends. "I thought leaving BC and Caddock at home meant I wouldn't have to deal with idiotic twats. Yet, here you two are taking the mickey out of everything."

"Is Remi the idiot or the twat?" Taine asked after a prolonged silence. "Just for clarification purposes."

Rubbing his forehead with a groan, Scottie couldn't help joining his friends in their laughter. Being at Castle Craig had been all about focus, quiet, and calm, three things he wasn't particularly skilled at doing. He appreciated all the help, but he was genuinely ecstatic to find some semblance of normalcy, without the getting absolutely sloshed every night and hopefully without the constant mind-numbing rage.

"Brought your mobile." Taine tossed it up to him. "I had to turn it off because it wouldn't stop buzzing all night."

Since Scottie's release came in the morning, his friends had driven up a few days earlier. The two had gone to visit Taine's adoptive father for a day before making their way to the castle. They'd all wanted to get an early start on the trip back to Cardiff.

Turning on his phone, Scottie was stunned to find over sixty calls and messages from his family. *What the fuck?* He scrolled through the increasingly panicked texts, ignoring the voicemail altogether. Those would be better listened to in private without his eavesdroppers hanging on every word.

The general gist of the messages all indicated his father had gotten sick. They didn't say with what, most just focused on calling Scottie an arse for not responding. *Fucking typical.* He decided to drop by his dad's place once he arrived in Cardiff.

Scrolling through all notes from his family, Scottie found the most recent text came from Gray. It wished him a safe journey home. He pressed his lips together to keep from grinning.

Over the course of his treatment, Gray had been the one to visit him most frequently during visiting hours on the weekends. Given the six-hour journey, Scottie hadn't really expected anyone to come up to see him. His friends—and Gray—had surprised him a great deal.

Gray: Have any plans for supper?

Scottie: Making sure my flat hasn't been broken into or destroyed.

Gray: It hasn't. I rode by it a few times a week to make certain.

Scottie: Nosy fucker.

Gray: You're welcome. Be at my place for supper at 8pm.

Scottie: Most people get asked out for a meal. Not told.

Gray: We're not most people.

CHAPTER EIGHT

GRAY

In the three months of Scottie's absence, Gray had built Ruck's reputation impressively well. The restaurant had a waiting list every night it was open. He'd even expanded the hours to include a few prized lunch spots a couple times a week.

Staffing had initially been a concern for him, but Akash had offered up a wise piece of advice. Gray worked with one of the Cardiff culinary courses to set up a work program. He hired students in his kitchen on a quarterly rotation, allowing them to fulfil some of the requirements for their certification.

To his mind, Gray considered it another way to pay forward a kindness once offered to him. He enjoyed the youthful enthusiasm—most of the time. They were often filled to the brim with new ideas, and he allowed them to follow their noses in experimenting.

Another new routine in his life was Alice and Alex, autistic twins who'd once worked at Akash's bakery. They'd begun working with Wyatt's botanist husband, Aled, in his garden down the street from Gray's cottage. Almost every morning the two stopped by his house for breakfast.

Alex had become obsessed with Gray's old Harley-Davidson. The young man had watched him work on the engine for a while and developed a keen interest. After a month or so, he'd gone out and bought himself a beat-up old Triumph, which they were fixing up together.

Somehow in moving to Cardiff, Gray had managed to unofficially adopt twins. He comforted himself with the knowledge that they were already grown. He did wonder how Scottie would take to the new development. Alice and Alex might help the former rugby player in his continued efforts to regain control of his life.

Pushing thoughts of all the recent changes in his life out of his mind, Gray focused on finishing up the last course for his diners. When they'd all gone, he shut down Ruck for the evening and sent his staff home. He had just enough time to prepare supper for Scottie.

Rushing through preparing pork chops and potatoes to go on a sheet pan in the oven, Gray had barely enough time to hop into the shower to wash away the grime of the day. He soaped up his hands and ran the suds over his body, reminding himself to be patient when his cock hardened to the touch while thinking about Scottie. A heavy knock on his front door had him hopping out of the shower and quickly wrapping a towel around his waist. He padded through the cottage, leaving wet footprints in his wake.

"Do you always answer the door fucking starkers?" Scottie stood on the stoop with his helmet under one arm. "Not sure everyone would appreciate the view as much as I am."

Taking the helmet away and setting it inside the door, Gray wrapped his fingers around Scottie's throat and gripped his short hair tightly with his other hand to drag him into a hard kiss. His hard shaft rubbed against the towel. He guided them into the dark shadows of the entryway.

"Out here? Honestly? Where all your neighbours can see us?" Scottie was already reaching between them to slip a hand through the opening of the towel to grasp Gray's cock. "I fucking missed you."

"Good. On your knees, like a good boy." Gray shoved Scottie down to the ground, shamelessly dropping his towel, glad for his foresight in not turning on the front lights. "Why don't we have a little teaser before supper? Work up an appetite for both of us. Show me how much you missed me, kitten."

Scottie glared up at him before his eyes dropped to the shaft bumping into his face. "If we get arrested…."

"We won't." Gray grabbed the wooden railing behind him when Scottie lunged forward to hungrily take an impressive portion of his cock into his mouth. "*Fuck.* Good boy."

With a herculean effort, Gray managed to remain silent. He'd no interest in drawing attention to them with him in such a vulnerable position. *Fuck. He's gifted with his mouth.*

Now was definitely not the time for a drawn-out encounter. Gray focused his attention on fully immersing himself into the sensations from the lips and tongue that he'd greatly missed as well. Scottie brought his hand up to play with his balls, but Gray smacked it away.

"Don't fucking move," Gray hissed quietly, before pulling himself out of the irresistible mouth. He stroked his cock until the evidence of his enjoyment covered Scottie's face. "Why don't you head inside to clean up? I'm sure by the time the evening is over we'll find new and enjoyable ways to dirty you all up again."

"Arse," Scottie grumbled. He got to his feet and froze mid-step when Gray grasped his cock firmly through his jeans. "*Fuck.*"

Grabbing his towel from the ground, Gray flicked Scottie in the arse with it and sent him into the house. They cleaned up in the bathroom, jostling for space at the sink. He eventually forced him up against the edge of it for a series of bruising kisses that left both of them gasping for air.

"Wasn't there supposed to be food?" Scottie dragged a towel across his face to dry it off.

"Fuck. *Supper.*" Gray got the pork chops out of the oven a few seconds away from them being burnt. "Well, at least they're not crispy."

Scottie joined him in the kitchen after rinsing himself off. He was clad only in his boxers and a T-shirt. He nicked a piece of potato from the tray. "I'm thrilled it's not fucking healthy shit. I learnt a lot of good stuff at the castle, but a little fat and grease aren't going to hurt me."

While they stood in the kitchen, Gray brought the conversation around to a topic that had been delayed by Scottie's absence. He didn't want any misunderstandings between them. Whatever this was between them, the rules would be well defined before emotions became too complicated.

With a blunt honesty, Gray covered his unique preferences and expectations. They'd discussed it briefly before, but not enough for his liking. On top of his list was his insistence that they both have complete check-ups to ensure they were healthy, not negotiable in his mind.

Gray's eyes turned stormy while he emphasised his zero tolerance for inviting others to join them in play. "I don't fucking share my toys, kitten. *Ever.*"

Through supper, they talked over hard limits. Gray respected Scottie's dislikes and expected the same in return. It was a relief to find the majority of their desires lined up perfectly.

When in a scene, Gray expected to always be in control. He was Sir. Scottie's job was to obey and to communicate honestly when he was uncomfortable or needed things to stop. Neither of them wanted to ever cross lines with each other.

Safe, sane, and consensual.

Gray waited until they'd finished up eating for the most important question. "Would you enjoy a tour of the playroom, kitten?"

Scottie grabbed his cup of water and choked half of it down before giving a hoarsely muttered, "Yes."

When Gray had made the move to Cardiff, he'd selected a cottage with enough space to have an entire room dedicated to his particular brand of sexual pleasure. It contained a host of toys, furniture, and other implements dedicated to his and his partner's enjoyment.

The prime feature of the den was the triangle cross set up on the right side of the room. Gray preferred it to the more traditional St. Andrew's version, believing it offered more comfort and flexibility. In his mind, ensuring the safety of his partner in a scene was paramount to anything else.

The room featured a bed specifically purchased for its sturdy wooden posts. *Functional and secure.* The closet held a toy chest along with a number of whips and paddles hanging from hooks. It also contained several loops of rope and a whole host of other things they'd eventually dabble with together.

Not wanting to throw too much at Scottie during their first scene, Gray opted for two of his favourite things—restraint and sensation play. After double checking his partner was still clear to play, he got Scottie naked and situated on his back on the bed. His legs were spread wide and his ankles secured to the posts with rope; his wrists were restrained by handcuffs to the headboard. The last addition was one of his preferred gags—it contained a moveable and detachable dildo, which he'd introduce to his sub in a few minutes.

Standing back to admire his handiwork, Gray headed down to the kitchen to grab a few of the ice frost massagers from his fridge. One contained a liquid centre that could be frozen, along with a vibrator; the other worked almost like a push pop when filled with water and left in the freezer. He intended to use them both to tease his captive.

With the non-vibrating massager in one hand, Gray slowly ran the frozen nub across Scottie's lower abdomen. He smirked when Scottie jumped at the sensation. Their eyes locked while he danced the ice up the tensed muscles to circle already hardened nipples.

"Fuck," Scottie groaned when the frozen toy was held firmly against his sensitive nub.

"What have I said about talking?" Gray picked up the slender dildo and guided it through the ring in the gag and between his lips. He reached over to take a dog clicker from a nearby nightstand to place it in Scottie's hand. "Press that if you want to stop. Nod if you understand, kitten."

After seeing the quick nod, Gray began to drilling the dildo in and out of Scottie's mouth, relishing in the muffled moans while dragging the massager across his cock. Pushing it out until the slender rod of ice was almost completely exposed; he decided to test it further down with the assistance of waterproof lubricant. His sub bucked as far as the restraints would allow when it was pressed into him.

Slowly easing it in and out of Scottie, Gray grabbed the second iced massager. He flicked the switch to cause it to vibrate. His cock grew painfully hard at the muffled moans coming from his captive as he feathered the toy across his nipples.

The rod inevitably melted away with the heat from Scottie's body. Gray slipped a finger in to replace it. His gaze stayed on the brown eyes that never drifted far away from his. It allowed them to feel connected by more than just the lone digit.

Even though Scottie held the clicker, Gray still watched carefully for any signs of physical or mental discomfort. Any scene should be enjoyed fully by both the Dominant and submissive. A Dom's job was to bring depths of raw pleasure to Scottie that the man had never experienced—to help him toe the lines in his own mind while respecting his limits.

Ragged breathing aside, his bound sub showed an intense level of eagerness for more. Scottie tried his hardest to press himself against the finger teasing him, straining against the restraints. Gray made a meal out of preparing him more, out of a sadistic desire to prolong the agony of not being allowed more than any actual necessity.

Grunting around the gag in his mouth, Scottie narrowed his eyes when yet another finger was added. His impatience spoke volumes even without him being able to say a word. Gray finally withdrew his hand and shifted up on the mattress.

After sliding on a condom, Gray made himself at home between Scottie's widely spread legs. He inched his lubed cock into his new sub while continuing to piston the dildo in and out of his mouth. Wanting to hear him fully, Gray yanked the gag out and tossed it aside.

They wouldn't kiss, not this time. Gray wanted Scottie to be painfully aware of who was in control of every aspect of the scene. He drove into him hard enough to shake the solid wood bed frame. *Fuck. I've waited so damn long for this.*

Working a hand between their bodies, Gray alternated between stroking Scottie's cock and squeezing it at the base tightly to prevent him from coming just yet. His thrusts were hard and fast while his stroking was slow and teasing. *I am a cruel son of a bitch.* He stopped several times to continue edging Scottie almost to the point of breaking before finally allowing both of them the satisfaction of climax.

"Holy fuck," Scottie gasped out after a few minutes. He hadn't moved aside from stretching his arms out after the restraints were removed. "Holy fucking fuck."

"Think you can walk, kitten? I want to get us cleaned up." Gray gently massaged Scottie's legs to ensure they hadn't cramped up from being restrained. "You good?"

"Fuck," Scottie repeated. "More than fucking good."

Gray couldn't help smirking down at him. He got slowly to his feet, discarding the condom in the nearby trash can, and moved over to the mini refrigerator in the right corner of the room to grab two bottles of water. "Here. Drink up. We'll grab a quick bite to eat after we shower."

Every aspect of the lifestyle was important to Gray, including aftercare. This was new to Scottie. They'd learn together what worked best for him post scene.

Following a quick shower and a midnight snack, it seemed wise to get some sleep, even if it felt like his alarm went off seconds after their heads hit the pillows. Gray left Scottie snoring in bed to go for his morning run. The twins had a habit of showing up early for breakfast, and he had no intention of being naked underneath the covers when they arrived.

He'd run, showered, dressed, and already started on breakfast when Scottie finally awoke. The twins arrived a few moments after. Alice snagged a piece of toast and tea before disappearing with her headphones on and her origami paper; her brother took the plate Gray offered into the living room and began pulling out a stack of magazines from his bag.

"Lad's going to fancy you." Scottie smirked over the rim of his mug of coffee and pointed to where Alex had spread out his books and magazines on motorbikes. "It won't take much."

"Doubtful, as he's not only asexual but aromantic, not that it's any business of yours." Gray sent a warning glare at Scottie.

"What the fuck is aromantic?"

"The short version is that he's not interested in either sex or romance." Gray didn't feel the need to go into it in depth, but he wanted to make it clear to Scottie to leave Alex alone. "And don't be a dick about it. His stepdad traumatised the poor kid enough as it is."

"I wouldn't. What? I wouldn't. I might be a complete arsehole, but I wouldn't do that to him." Scottie set his mug aside to head over to Alex; he crouched down across from where the young man sat on the floor. "What are you working on?"

Well, here's hoping the last three months actually taught him something useful and he doesn't terrify Alex.

CHAPTER NINE

SCOTTIE

BC: Oi. Have a second?

Scottie: I'm busy working. Fuck off.

BC: Wanking to porn at your desk isn't work.

Scottie: What do you want Boyce?

BC: Don't be testy. We've decided to have a charity rugby match with some of the lads that Tens coaches. Want to join in? We'll have a practice next weekend.

Scottie: Aren't you worried about breaking a hip?

BC: Don't be an arse. Are you in or not?

Scottie: Fuck. Fine. Not like we haven't had enough humiliation in our lives to last a lifetime. We might want to practice more than once if we're going to even attempt to demonstrate our skills.

BC: First, I have to convince Remi and Caddock.

Scottie: I'll talk to Remi.
BC: That's a shit idea.

It was a terrible idea, but Scottie had made a promise to himself not to take his friends for granted. *Can I be less a fucking wanker?* Probably not, but at the least, he could attempt to be a bit nicer.

Rehab hadn't changed him or his enjoyment of beer. He'd never actually been addicted to drinking it. Booze had been his anaesthesia to numb his pain, anger, and memories.

Rehab hadn't helped solve that—it had provided a place to clear his mind. Therapy had. Or maybe, more accurately, it had required both.

Detox had offered a clarity while also exposing his rage and hurt. Three months of the hardest work Scottie had ever done in his life. He'd made a promise to himself not to throw away the peace he'd found.

I'm still an arsehole, but at least I'm a calm one.

To his surprise, surrendering himself to Gray settled something in him even more than rehab had done. For all the restraints, Scottie was the one in control. A single word from him would bring things to a screeching halt, and somehow that knowledge allowed him to relax into the safety of Gray's strength without feeling embarrassed by his craving for it.

"Scottie?"

He froze in the process of getting off his bike outside of his flat and glanced around for a moment. "Silus?"

His younger half-brother waved at him with a sheepish grin from where he sat cross-legged on a nearby bench with a book in his lap. They had the same father—different mothers.

Silus's mum had been wise enough to run far away from the Monk insanity. As a result, Scottie rarely saw the twenty-four-year-old, though they emailed frequently.

"You were thirteen, ugly, and freckled the last time I saw you. Haven't fucking changed much." Scottie threw his arm around his brother's neck to drag him closer. "Heard you graduated from the Imperial College with top honours."

"You'd know since you sent Mum the money for it," Silus teased. He'd gotten their dad's looks but his mother's slight frame, darker skin, and thankfully, her personality. "I'll never understand why you wanted it to be a secret."

"Fuck off." Scottie dragged him toward the stairs up to his flat. He'd never wanted his half-brother to feel indebted to him. "One of his Monk bastards should do something with their brains. You're our best chance."

"Only chance." Silus wiggled away from him with a snicker. "How've you been? I was worried when Mum said you went to rehab."

"Better. Sober, mostly. All the time actually. Dead boring." He headed into the kitchen to put the kettle on. "Want a coffee?"

"Sure." His brother hopped onto the counter, setting his book next to him. "Mum said you've found a boyfriend."

Scottie shot a warning glare over at him. "How does she know that?"

"Ha! I knew it." Silus swung his legs out of the way of the kick Scottie aimed at him. "Tricked you."

"Little fucker."

Silus took a letter out of his pocket and waved it at him.

"Guess who was accepted into the computing postgraduate program at Cardiff Metropolitan University."

"Congrats." Scottie exchanged the letter for a mug of coffee. "And a scholarship. Fucking brilliant."

"I know." Silus set the coffee on top of his book and pulled his phone out of his pocket. "Have you heard from Dad?"

Scottie lowered the letter to frown at his brother. "Don't let him mess with you, kid. You hear me? Don't let him screw with your head."

"He's dying."

Scottie let the letter fall out of his suddenly slack fingers. "What the fuck?"

"Cirrhosis."

Scottie rubbed his fingers across his face, suddenly feeling exhausted and in serious need of an entire bottle of whisky. *No, that's not going to help anything.* "Fuck."

"Yeah." Silus lifted his shoulders in a shrug. His hazel eyes met Scottie's hesitantly. "What do we do?"

"You focus on your university shit." Scottie refused to allow their father to derail Silus even for a second, even if he was at death's door. The bastard wouldn't get the chance to ruin another kid's life. "Let me know when you're moving out, and I'll give you a hand."

"Fine. *Fine.* You'll keep me updated. Promise, Scottie? I have a right to know." Silus glared at him with a stubbornness that was all too familiar. "And I haven't forgotten your little attempt to disrupt the conversation. I want to hear all about this boyfriend."

Scottie decided not to waste his energy warning his brother

off; he was a Monk after all, and unlikely to listen. "How about we have supper at Ruck next week?"

"Ruck?"

"Where else are you going to meet the chef?"

"Wait. You're dating the chef at Ruck?" Silus grinned before taking a sip of his coffee. "What's he like?"

"American."

CHAPTER TEN

GRAY

Fuck.

How long are the fucking memories going to plague me?

Waking up with the taste of copper in his mouth and the acrid smell of gunpowder in his nose, Gray shot up and sank back into the pillows with a tired sigh. He finally shifted around to sit on the edge of the bed. A few shakes of his head brought him out of the last of the haze of his nightmare.

Over ten years after his return from war, Gray still occasionally fought with the demons that haunted his memories. Old Sam would've called it shell shock. *PTSD.* That was what they called it now. All the experts recommended a different solution; he'd opted to throw his emotional upheaval into morning runs, cooking, and sex. It wouldn't work for everyone, but it had for him.

With another tired sigh, Gray pushed himself to his feet and decided to run off the lingering remnants of the nightmare. He pulled on socks, shorts, and an old USMC T-shirt before shoving his feet into running shoes. The narrow, winding roads around his cottage always managed to sort through any thoughts weighing on his mind.

He stepped outside and glanced down in surprise to find Scottie sitting on the ground with his back against the wall near the door. "What the fuck are you doing? Why didn't you knock? Come to think of it, how long have you been here?"

Scottie peered up at him with tired eyes that were reddened and slightly swollen. "Dunno."

"Right." Gray decided if a run helped him, it might help Scottie. He reached down to yank the man up to his feet. "Let's go for a walk. Sitting on your ass isn't going to help."

"Arse."

"Ass." Gray locked his door and shoved Scottie forward toward the road. "Get your *ass* in gear."

"Arse," Scottie corrected with exaggerated enunciation "*You're* an arse."

"Americans." Scottie fell silent as they moved further down the road.

As Scottie seemed incapable of either running or speaking, Gray opted for a slow walk out of his little neighbourhood. They'd gone almost a mile onto the hiking path that went through the dense forest when the man at his side veered off toward a clump of trees. Scottie slammed his fist into one of the trunks before resting his forehead against the bark.

"I've found punching hard surfaces rarely does anything

to help aside from possibly breaking bones." Gray leaned against one of the other nearby trees. "Want to talk about it?"

Scottie collapsed onto a tree stump, shoulders slumping forward while he dragged his fingers roughly over his head. "Heard from my brother."

"You have a brother?"

"I probably have more than one. I'd wager there's a tonne of little Monk bastards running around the country. I've only ever known the one for certain. He's a half-brother, actually. I tried to look out for him without actually fucking his life up with all my shit." Scottie grabbed a branch from off the ground and began to absently strip it of leaves while he spoke. "He's in his twenties. Smart. Nice. Nothing like me."

"You have your moments." Gray moved over to a second fallen tree to sit down. "What'd he have to say?"

"Dad's dying." Scottie snapped the branch in his hands in half. "Turns out he's got both cirrhosis of the liver and cancer as well."

"Fuck."

"The bastard ignored all of the symptoms for months. His doctor suggested surgery and a transplant, but he refused to be put on the list. He apparently doesn't want to have to quit drinking." Scottie grabbed another branch off the ground and started the process of peeling it bare. "He's trying to guilt Silus, my brother, into caring for him since he'll be living in Cardiff soon. I won't let him mess up another one of his kids' lives while he's at the tail end of his own."

"Ahh."

"Should just shove him into the bay and have done with it." Scottie stared morosely down at the twig in his hands;

he clenched it tightly enough his fingers whitened, and the wood crumbled. "I couldn't give two shits about the bastard. He never did a thing for me, but…."

"But?"

"What if when he dies, I find myself with a million fucking regrets and no chance for closure?" He brushed his fingers off on his jeans and slumped forward to bury his face in his hands. "I talked to my counsellor about it yesterday when I found myself wanting to chug down a few bottles of whisky. This is what he does to me. I've no interest in stumbling into that trap again."

Gray shifted forward until he could rest his hand on the back of Scottie's neck, gently massaging the tense muscles. "Regrets are a son of a bitch."

Only the slight shrug of his shoulder indicated that Scottie had heard him. Gray continued to stroke his neck soothingly, a small comfort but hopefully one to ground him until his thoughts settled. He could understand on several levels the conflicting emotions at play.

"What are you going to do?" Gray asked after ten minutes of silence.

"Try to care for him as best I can and hopefully not lose my mind in the process." Scottie twisted his head to the side to face him. "What else can I do? Silus can't afford to take time off from university—he'd lose his scholarship. I'd hire someone, but who knows what the old bastard would do to a nurse. The hazard pay might bankrupt me."

Gray squeezed his neck firmly. "You've got friends. You're not alone."

"Yeah."

"You've got me as well." Gray had no intention of letting his newly found partner and sub collapse under the weight of what he preferred to call *familial horseshit*. "C'mon. We'll finish hiking, and then I'll make breakfast."

"And fuck?" Scottie chuckled weakly when Gray swatted him on the back of the head. "Taking that as a yes."

"Of course you are." Gray got to his feet and dragged Scottie up with him. "We'll see. Not sure I should indulge you in an emotionally compromised state of mind."

"Fuck you."

"Be a good boy, and I just might fuck you." He grabbed Scottie firmly by the arse, squeezing hard and pushing him toward the path. "Keep walking."

CHAPTER ELEVEN

SCOTTIE

"Doesn't your friend Tens know a nurse intimately?" Gray had the newspaper spread across the table in front of them while they sat side by side at the island in the kitchen an hour later, eating breakfast. "Ruck made the paper."

"Brilliant." Scottie paused with a fork full of omelette halfway to his mouth. "A nurse? *Right*. Freddie. How the fuck did I forget about him?"

"Would he help?"

"Probably." Scottie dropped the fork onto the plate as his appetite suddenly fled. "Not sure Tens would thank me for foisting my bastard of a father onto his Freddie. I'm pretty sure he'd kick my arse from Cardiff to London and back at least twice before drowning me in the river."

"He might have suggestions for what you can do." Gray stretched his arm out to grab the coffee pot from the nearby counter to top up their mugs. "Would your dad even take professional help?"

"From his violent reaction to the doctor? I doubt it. He's happy enough to drink himself to death." Scottie shoved his plate away, suddenly nauseated by the smell of eggs. He stared morosely down at the paper without reading a word. "I could drop kick him for doing this to me."

Shaking his head with a bitter laugh, Scottie could admit to himself he wasn't being fair. For all his faults, his father hadn't drunk himself halfway into the grave to spite him. He knew the next few months or years wouldn't be easy.

His father wouldn't follow any of the doctor's suggestions. Bringing Freddie into it might not do anything but exacerbate a difficult situation and bring the wrath of Taine down on his head. But it couldn't hurt to ask the nurse for advice.

Right?

"Send Freddie a text. It can't hurt to ask." Gray folded up the paper and tossed it aside, getting to his feet when a quiet knock interrupted their breakfast. "Ahh, the twins. I was wondering if we'd see them this morning."

While Gray went to open the door, Scottie fished around in his pocket for his mobile. He stared down at it for several seconds. If he messaged Freddie, all of his friends would know about his dad.

Am I ready for their sympathy? What am I so fucking afraid of? Having my friends show they care about me?

One issue that had frequently come up in his therapy sessions was his inability to let others into his life. Scottie trusted his rugby brothers more than anyone else in his life—

Gray was slowly becoming a close second. His therapist thought he needed to learn how to let his friends in more often.

Scottie: Got a minute?

Taine: What's going on?

Scottie: Silus came to visit me.

Taine: Didn't know you kept in touch.

Scottie: He heard from my dad.

Taine: Shite.

Taine: What do you need?

Scottie: Some advice from your nicer half. If I promise not to be an arsehole, will you both have lunch with me today?

Taine: Why don't we ask Gray to set up a chef's table for us at Ruck? Guaranteed privacy and good food.

A quick conversation with Gray confirmed the man had no issues accommodating them. Ruck had a small space just off the kitchen that was set up specifically for a private chef's table. Scottie confirmed the time with Taine and told himself that he'd done the right thing.

Leaving Gray to his morning rituals with Alice and Alex, Scottie headed home. He wanted a hot shower and a change of clothes before baring his soul to his friends. It might go a long way toward settling him.

Taine: Remi said to give you a warning.

Scottie: Warning about what?

Taine: Zeb's in town.

Scottie: Why? Don't I have enough shit to deal with right now than a jumped-up cocky French fucker?

Taine: Cocky? That's a bit rich coming from you.

Taine: Remi said to play nicely.

Scottie: Again I say—fuck. Fuck off the lot of you and Remi in particular. And why didn't the elder Frenchie contact me directly?

Taine: He assumed you'd take it better coming from me.

Zeb Chardin had been a rival of his when they'd both played rugby internationally. He happened to be a bit younger, a bit more talented, and slightly nicer than Scottie, which meant he'd managed his career better. They'd gone head-to-head in a few matches when France had played the Lions.

Fuck.

With any luck, I'll be able to avoid the bastard.

How much luck have I actually had lately?

Fucking none.

That's how much.

Lunch with Taine and his boyfriend went relatively well. Freddie had immediately offered to send an email with suggestions for how to care for his dad, along with recommendations for how to find in-home help. Scottie had no idea if his old man would even go for any of it.

I'll be lucky if the stubborn arsehole even lets me in the door.

"About Zeb." Taine pulled Scottie outside of Ruck for an apparently private talk. They glared at each other for several seconds. "Look, give the lad a chance, will you?"

"Why?" Scottie had a distinct feeling whatever his old friend was about to say would make him want to take a swing at him, so he shoved his hands into his pockets. "What have you done now?"

"We thought you might want a bit of help at the club while you're dealing with your dad." Taine appeared to be bracing himself with his arms folded across his chest. "Zeb just finished up and has a few months free."

"No."

"Scottie."

"Fuck off. No, I'm not working with that smug wanker." Scottie scowled at Taine when he started to open his mouth. "And don't go off on how I'm a hypocrite."

"Consider it a test of your new state of mind." Taine smiled serenely when Scottie's glare intensified. "Give it a try. He's mellowed out a bit."

"Doubtful."

"You've mellowed out a bit as well," Taine reminded him.

"*Fuck.*" Scottie could only shake his head with a sigh of resignation. "Fine, but if we burn the place to the ground, I'm placing the blame firmly on your shoulders."

"Fair enough." Taine threw an arm around his shoulder to return to Ruck. "You know we're proud of you, right? We thought we'd be burying you, but you're turning your life around."

"Fuck off."

"You're welcome." Taine shoved him toward the door of the restaurant. "I am proud of you."

"But don't screw it up?" Scottie tried to play off his embarrassment with a joke, but his old rugby teammate wasn't having it.

"I'm proud of you." He stepped back to allow a few customers to exit before they re-entered Ruck. "Full stop."

CHAPTER TWELVE

GRAY

"What is she doing here?"

Gray froze in the middle of what he'd been doing to follow the maître d's eyes toward one of the new waitresses. "Yara came in to work early to help set up. Any problems?"

"No, sir." The young maître d' cowered at his glare and raced away.

With a nod to Yara, who smiled brightly at him, Gray made a mental note to keep an eye on the way the staff interacted with his newest server. Given his experiences as a kid, he had a zero-tolerance policy for bullying, whatever the reason. Anyone who tested him would quickly find themselves out of a job.

When Yara Stout had interviewed with him for the job, Gray had been impressed with her personality and her CV.

He'd offered the position, not fazed at all by the buttons on her jacket that proudly proclaimed her pronouns along with what he thought was a Trans flag. She'd gotten teary-eyed when he'd shrugged and welcomed her to the Ruck family, making him wonder how many restaurants had turned her away.

In all honesty, he admired her courage. After moving to Cardiff with her parents from Brazil to be closer to her mother's family, her father had kicked her out of the house at sixteen. An aunt had taken her in and cared for her ever since, though now at twenty she'd sought a job that might pay better to help with the bills.

Good kid.

Wonder if she'd enjoy meeting Alice and Alex?

They like quiet people, and she's like a mouse.

For much of the day after lunch, Scottie played sentinel in the kitchen. Gray often looked up in the midst of cooking to find him brooding in the corner. He wanted to unravel whatever spiral of thought had gotten him into such a morose state, but customers, unfortunately, had to be served first.

Dish after dish went out of the kitchen. The steady flow of servers in out and out appeared to trigger Scottie's hair trigger. Gray had no intention of allowing him to lash out at his employees.

"Stupid little—" Scottie snarled at one of the staff who'd bumped into him accidentally.

Gray grabbed him by the shoulder to guide him away from the young server. "I know you're angry and messed up in the head about your father, but don't fall back on your habit of taking it out on those around you. Don't make me punish you, kitten. On second thought, go ahead. I'd love to have you bent over a chair, bared for my pleasure."

"Fucker."

Gray forced him to turn around and shoved him toward the door at the opposite end of the kitchen. "Go hang out in my office for a bit to calm yourself."

After finishing the last of the cleaning, Gray sent the employees home, locked up Ruck, and checked in on Scottie. He found him slouched on the two-seat sofa that rested against the wall across from his desk. From his furrowed brow, it didn't appear the time alone had done anything to help.

"Want to talk about it?" Gray perched on the edge of his desk with his arms across his chest while he stared down at Scottie. "Is it just about your old man?"

"Mostly." Scottie sat up and stretched his legs out in front of him. His shoes knocked against Gray's. "*Fuck.* The bastard has always managed to cause issues for me."

"What do you need?" Gray watched Scottie's eyes drift to the bottle of whisky sitting on a nearby bookshelf. "Not going to drown yourself in booze, are you?"

Scottie shook his head slowly and purposefully forced his gaze to Gray. "It's tempting, though."

"What do *you* need, kitten?" Gray had no doubts a scene would do wonders for shaking Scottie from his mood, but wanted him to be the one to ask. "You'll have to ask nicely."

With the results of their medical tests coming in clean, Gray had found himself eagerly anticipating their next scene. *How far can I push the kitten?* Discovering a sub's boundaries was always his favourite type of adventure. *Is he really ready for a deeper exploration? Only one way to find out.*

Scottie glowered at him while the silence stretched between them. "Fuck you."

Gray canted his head to the side, allowing his gaze to drift slowly up and down Scottie's body. He could see how close to the edge he was. "No, but maybe I'll fuck you if you beg me to."

"Not a chance," Scottie scoffed.

Gray's lips twisted into a wicked smile. "You've begged for me before, kitten. It was beautiful music to my ears."

"Fuck off."

The two words were far softer than Scottie usually voiced them. Gray couldn't make the decision for his sub; the act of submission, in his opinion, happened each time they came together. He waited and watched patiently for the man slouched on the sofa to make up his mind.

He believed, as a Dominant, that waiting to be asked was a critical start to foreplay, but also a signal of consent. His job was to stretch a submissive's limits without betraying their trust. The real power lay in Scottie's hands; one "no" and the party ended immediately.

"I can't—" Scottie shut his mouth so sharply it had to hurt.

Gray enjoyed greatly the obvious internal struggle going on in front of him. "Yes, you can. Find the words like a good boy."

A visible shudder went through Scottie. Gray's dick hardened at the sight of clear evidence of his words affecting the man. He shifted slightly on the desk to make the bulge evident.

Scottie's eyes almost instantly dropped down to his crotch. "*Fuck.*"

"Ask nicely, kitten," Gray reiterated. He dropped his hand to his cock to casually stroke himself through his trousers. "You remember how."

And he did.

After a minute or two of continued internal debate, Scottie slid off the sofa to the floor. His jaw clenched tightly enough that Gray wanted to massage his own in sympathetic pain. His sub's hand stretched out toward him before dropping back to his side.

"Good boy. You always wait for permission before touching." Gray feathered his fingers across Scottie's furrowed brow. "Ready to ask?"

Scottie opened and closed his mouth several times. He seemed frozen in place for a full minute. "Can I touch you, sir?"

Gray caught Scottie by the neck to press him forcefully into his cloth-covered cock. He watched as the tension slipped out of his submissive in his finally taking the step. "I'm proud of you."

Seeing as they weren't at his home in his well-equipped play den, Gray opted to improvise the scene. *Hell, I might use the damn office more often if it smells sweetly of Scottie's surrender.* He continued to rub his lover's face against his trousers until his hunger to get the man naked and stretched over the desk grew too strong to deny.

Getting to his feet, Gray yanked Scottie up and immediately shoved him face first onto the desk. It took no time at all to get both their trousers and briefs around their ankles. He pumped two of his fingers into Scottie's mouth, moistening them before moving down to roughly thrust them into his other favourite orifice—more for the tease than to prepare him.

The bare arse staring at him proved impossible to resist. A quick glance around the room helped him identify the perfect implement. *Why thank you, Francis, for including a wooden ruler amongst all the shit you purchased for the office.* Pressing Scottie's head down with a firm warning not to move, Gray dragged the edge of his improvised tool along the inside of his thigh up to the crease of his arse.

Careful not to overdo it, Gray heated Scottie's cheeks with precision born from years of practice. He made certain to gently caress the pinkened skin in between swats. By the time he was satisfied, Scottie had begun to practically hump the hard surface of the desk.

With one last swat and a command not to move again, Gray slicked his cock up and pressed in. He enjoyed the sharp intake of Scottie's breath. Intermingling swats to his sub's behind with hard thrusts, he drew out his enjoyment as long as possible, making sure to tightly wrap his fingers around Scottie's hard, leaking shaft to keep him from achieving climax.

"Your relief only comes when I say it does, kitten," Gray growled out the words before one final surge forward; he ruthlessly filled Scottie to the brim with his pleasure. "Fuck."

"Sir?" Scottie bit the word out through heavy panting. "Please?"

Gray dragged his fingers down the taut muscles of

Scottie's back. "Jack off on the desk."

"The fuck?"

"Be a good kitten. Not sure your ass can handle another punishment." Gray flicked one cheek lightly. "I want to watch you do it."

"*Fucker.*" Scottie hissed when Gray swatted him again. "Yes, sir."

Pulling up his own clothes, Gray reclined on the sofa to watch the show. Scottie's gaze locked on his Dominant's while his fingers wrapped firmly around his cock and stroked quickly. It didn't take much for him to climax across the desk.

"Lick it clean, kitten. *Now.*" Gray leaned forward to run his fingers along the still slightly pinked cheeks when Scottie bent over with muttered cursing. He breathed a quiet sigh as he noticed his submissive's tense shoulders had relaxed. The scene had worked the magic he'd hoped. "Good boy."

CHAPTER THIRTEEN

SCOTTIE

Scottie stood in the alley outside of his dad's place, staring up at the curtained windows. He'd been there for long enough he was surprised the nosy bint next door hadn't called the police. "What the fuck am I doing?"

"Talking to yourself. Old age getting to you?" Silus stepped up beside him on the pavement. "Going in?"

"What are you doing here? Didn't I tell you to leave the old bastard to me?" Scottie glared at his younger brother. "Did he call you again and try to guilt trip you into coming over?"

Silus rolled his eyes and gave an exaggerated sigh. "I'm not fourteen, Scottie. He's just as much my father as he is yours."

"He hasn't fucked you up yet." Scottie would go to great lengths to keep his half-brother far away from the toxic bastard.

"Don't let him."

Silus caught him by the arm and pushed until Scottie turned to face him. "One of these days, you'll stop giving him the power to keep you all messed up inside. Is he a right arsehole? Definitely. Am I glad Mum protected me from him? Oh yes, more than I can ever express to her. You're stronger than he is, Scottie, and stronger than the memories of all the abuse in your childhood. Maybe Monks are drunken bastards, but we don't have to be."

"I'm sober."

"Yes, but you're still a bit of a bastard. Work on that, will you?" Silus danced out of reach of the swing of Scottie's arm. "Why don't we go see him together? He's usually nicer to me."

"Think he's scared of your mum."

"C'mon, you big coward." Silus grabbed him by the sleeve of his shirt to attempt to lead him toward the door. "You're heavier than a hippo."

"Did you just call me fat, you little twerp?" Scottie threw his arm around Silus's neck to drag him over to muss up his hair. "Right. *Fine.* Let's go."

Opening the door, they trudged up the stairs toward the flat. Scottie exchanged a glance with Silus, who looked far more nervous than he had outside. He wrapped an arm around his younger sibling's shoulder and reached out with his other hand to bang on the door.

Nothing.

Hope the fucker's not dead.

Silus elbowed him in the side. "Stop thinking uncharitable thoughts."

"Stop listening to your mum's church lectures." Scottie earned another dig in his ribs that made him chuckle. He rapped his fist on the wooden door a second, and then third time. "Open up, you drunken bastard."

"*Scottie*," Silus snapped quietly. "Let's not start the conversation with a fight."

"Why? He's going to end it with one." Scottie had no doubts at all that any attempts to help their father would eventually lead to at least a verbal altercation. He had no intention of allowing the man to take any of his hatred out on Silus. "I'll do my best."

"Good." Silus grinned at him. "You're buying me lunch afterwards."

"Moocher." He turned back toward the door as it started to open, stepping forward slightly to allow himself more room to get between his father and his brother if necessary. "We've come to visit."

"Oh? No shit. Thought you'd come to sell me a vacuum." The eldest Monk glowered at the two of them before breaking off in a coughing fit. He shoved the hand that Scottie put out toward him. "Why are you two twits here? Didn't I tell you I don't need any of your help?"

"You're not well." Silus cut into the conversation, stopping Scottie from immediately starting into the man. "We want to help."

"Help me into my fucking grave? I'm already halfway there. And tell the brute of a nurse you hired for me that I'm not interested in my quality of fucking life. I'll drink and smoke as much as I sodding want to." He slammed the door shut in their face.

"Pleasant." Silus stared for a few minutes before turning toward Scottie. "So, lunch?"

Scottie rubbed a tired hand over his face with a wry chuckle. "Fine. Let's go to Ruck. You can meet Gray."

"Brilliant."

"You still driving the Ford Fiesta?" Scottie had tried to give his brother a new, less crap car, but he'd refused—Monk pride at its best. "Is it up for the drive to Ruck?"

"Don't be mean." Silus checked all of his pockets twice before finding his keys. "It's not bad for my first car. By the time I finish my courses, I'll find a great job working in IT, and I'll buy some fancy wheels for myself."

"You've duct taped the fucking mirror on your driver side." Scottie made a mental note to get the Fiesta to a garage whether his brother liked it or not. "I'll follow you just in case your tin can breaks down."

"Does it require practice to be this annoying, or is it a family trait I missed out on?" Silus fumbled with the keys before getting the door open. "Don't ride into a tree."

When they arrived at Ruck, the restaurant lot was almost full. Scottie guided his brother into one of the employee spots. The Sin Bin staff wouldn't show up for a few hours, so no one should mind.

And fuck them if they do.

Ruck appeared to be in the middle of a fully booked lunch tasting. Scottie glanced around the room and spotted familiar faces across the room at the table usually reserved for one of the owners. He caught Silus by the shoulder to guide him across the restaurant to introduce him to a few of his former teammates.

"Remi. When did you get into town?" Scottie gritted his teeth and forced himself to keep the smile on his face when he realised the Frenchie's idiot cousin sat at the table along with Sarah, Remi's wife, and her brother, Ivan. He introduced Silus to them as the only Monk with any brains, and left Zeb for last. "And this is Zippity Doo Da."

"Zeb. My name is Zeb." The smooth French rugby player stood to shake Silus's hand with a wink that left Silus grinning and Scottie irate. "It's a pleasure."

Scottie reined in his temper; he always tried to avoid showing the worst of himself to Silus. He opted to simply glower at Zeb instead. "Zippie."

Silus's grin widened, his attention solely focused on Zeb. "The pleasure is *all* mine."

Fuck.

Scottie turned his scowl on his brother and harshly whispered, "*No.*"

CHAPTER FOURTEEN

GRAY

War Hero Turned Executive Chef Or Disgraced Police Chief Fleeing Sordid Affair. The newspaper headline was as eye-catching as the article attached to it. When a journalist had asked to interview him about Ruck, Gray hadn't thought his history would be dragged into it.

On his morning run, Gray'd stopped to grab the morning paper. The black-and-white words taunted him mercilessly. He'd hoped an ocean separating him from his past would be sufficient.

Apparently not.

There was only a tiny paragraph covering Ruck and his food. The rest read like a scandalous tabloid rather than a restaurant review. He wondered how the five owners would take notoriety.

For his part, Gray'd never allowed the opinions of others to affect him greatly. The only good part of the article was the journalist had stuck to the facts without embellishing. He had to admit the story didn't really require exaggeration to be titillating.

Never the type to hide from anything, Gray decided to head into Ruck early. If the retired rugby players who owned it intended to fire him, they'd have to do it in person. He hoped they wouldn't, as Cardiff was growing on him.

Finishing up his breakfast and downing his coffee, Gray went outside and found Scottie leaning against his bike by the kerb. He had a paper in one hand and a wide grin on his face. Scottie must've driven up while he was in the shower and waited for him.

"Don't smirk, kitten," Gray said sharply.

"Welcome to the tabloid club." Scottie continued to grin at him. "I used to feature in at least one a week—drunk or naked, or both. Remi, BC, Tens, Caddock, and I managed to get photographed going for a naked dip in the ocean a while ago."

"I'm in questionable company, then." Gray narrowed his eyes when Scottie lifted the paper. "Kitten…."

Ignoring the warning, Scottie began to read the article. He seemed almost gleeful while recounting how Gray had been outed by a former submissive in the small town in Washington where he'd served as chief of police. *I should've trusted my instincts and stayed in bed this morning.*

The submissive in question had gotten into trouble and tried to use his relationship with the police chief to get out of it. Gray not only refused to help him, but ended things immediately. As revenge, the man had gone to the papers with proof of Gray's so-called deviance.

Conservative, small-town America hadn't reacted kindly to their police chief frequenting gay BDSM clubs in nearby towns. While they hadn't actually moved to fire him, Gray had decided to retire. He hadn't wanted to spend the remainder of his working years fighting a battle against bigots, even if it left his reputation in tatters.

He had no family alive to care, and his friends knew better than to pay attention to anything in a paper. Gray vividly recalled something Old Sam had once told him. *People are always going to try to rip you to shreds; you don't control them so best walk away and leave it be.*

"Oi. Are you ignoring me?" Scottie swatted him on the arm with the paper. "Rude American bastard."

Gray glanced down at the paper and up at Scottie before snatching it out of his hand. "In the house, kitten. I've got a more creative use for a rolled-up newspaper."

Scottie exhaled a hard, shuddering breath before lifting his eyes to meet Gray's gaze. "Sir?"

"Good boy. Now, get your ass in the house. I want you naked and on your knees in the play den." Gray followed at a leisurely pace while Scottie strode quickly into the cottage. "My morning's looking up."

Futzing around in the kitchen, Gray wasted time, wanting Scottie to be forced to wait on his own. He had no doubts his sub's mind had already started to race with what they might do. His fingers tightened the rolled-up paper while he contemplated his plan for the morning.

With time limited, it seemed imperative to carefully work to get the most out of the scene. Gray set the kitchen timer to give him a reminder. *Here's hoping I hear it.* He found Scottie naked on his knees with his eyes on the newest addition to the room—another cross, this one a take on the St. Andrew's, but shaped like an hourglass with several welded rings on the top, bottom, and middle.

Gray dropped his hand on Scottie's head, roughly dragging his fingers across the short hair. "Are you excited, kitten?"

Scottie nodded sharply.

"Use your words." Gray gripped the short hairs to yank Scottie's head back. "Are you excited?"

Scottie cleared his throat and ran his tongue over his bottom lip before finally answering. "Yes, sir."

"Good boy." Gray dragged him up into a kiss before releasing him. "On your feet."

Once Scottie stood up, Gray pushed him toward the cross. He stroked his sub's already half-hard shaft to a full erection and slipped a ring around it. The second part of the contraption went around his balls; it would be highly entertaining to see the response when he realised the knobbed plastic denied him completion while at the same time vibrating him in a constant tease.

Leaving the cock ring switched off for the moment, Gray arranged Scottie in front of the wooden structure. He spread first his arms and then his legs, connecting him by the wrists and ankles to metal rings with metal cuffs. His fingers danced along the insides of his sub's thighs before ensuring he was both securely and safely fastened.

"Fuck." Scottie bucked slightly against the cross when Gray nudged his balls with the side of the newspaper before slipping a slender plug into his arse. "*Fuck,* sir."

"You know better than to speak." Gray tapped him again, harder this time, in the same sensitive spot. "Time to punish you for your smirking."

After ensuring his submissive was clear to continue, Gray took a moment to undress. He carefully draped his clothing across the nearby bookshelf. With the position of the cross, Scottie could only hear the movements without being able to see anything.

Ahh, anticipation.

Not wanting to draw the moment out longer, Gray went in for the first swat with relish. He caught Scottie with the paper on his left cheek before moving to the other side of his arse. Time flew as he methodically alternated his spanking to pause periodically to check on his submissive and also to turn on the vibration on the cock ring.

A steady stream of moaning punctuated each hit. Gray reached around to wrap his fingers around Scottie's shaft. He bit down on the pinkened skin, eliciting an expletive-laced babble from his submissive that turned into him begging for release.

"Not yet. Be a good boy." Gray worked methodically until he had Scottie teetering on the edge of coherency. He tossed the paper to the side and rested his hand gently on the warmed skin. "Can't wait to fuck you like this."

One last swat with his hand silenced Scottie before he

could get a word out. Gray yanked out the plug, tossing it to the side and sliding his shaft in to replace it. He rested his forehead against his sub's sweaty back to enjoy the tightness surrounding him.

With one hand, Gray reached around to begin stroking Scottie in time with his thrusts. He moved slowly, intent on fully enjoying the submissive trussed up at his mercy. His kitten had his hands clenched into fists against the wood, and he begged for release.

Not yet.

Gray refused to make it too easy for his submissive. He used his years of experience to draw out his own climax as long as possible. His fingers gripped the sensitive flesh of Scottie's arse while he continued to ride him hard.

"Please?" Scottie's voice took on an edge of desperation.

Stopping his stroking of Scottie's cock only increased his begging. Gray carefully removed the cock ring, dropping it to the floor and picking up where he'd stopped. He worked them both to release that left him panting for air, and his submissive slumped against the restraints.

Well, fuck.

We're definitely going to be late for the meeting.

Easing himself out, Gray kicked the cock ring to the side and began to release Scottie from the cross. He kept an arm around Scottie to help him toward the en-suite. They both needed a shower; his submissive would also need some lotion for his warmed bottom if he were to be able to sit anytime soon.

Instead of a shower, they had a warm bath. The mild water

soothed Scottie from his first real spanking from Gray. Despite his gruff grumbling, he settled into his arms in the water and dozed.

When the water cooled too much, Gray forced them both out of the bath. He ordered Scottie face first into the bed and gently lotioned his arse. Leaving him for a minute, he retrieved a few bottles of water and a packet of leftover sandwiches from the fridge.

"Hungry?" Gray placed a sandwich on the bed next to Scottie along with a bottle. "I'd recommend eating on your side if possible until the lotion dries."

"You're wasting time." Scottie shifted on the mattress slightly but grabbed a sandwich when Gray stared at him. "What's the point of all this shit?"

"Aftercare. Get used to it." Gray dragged the cold bottle of water across one of Scottie's bare cheeks, smirking when he hissed at the sensation. "Maybe a bit more lotion before we leave for Ruck."

"*Bastard.*"

CHAPTER FIFTEEN

SCOTTIE

From the smirk on Gray's face, Scottie knew the man had heard his slight hiss of discomfort when he sat on his bike. *Bastard.* Both the bath and lotion had reduced the tenderness significantly; only a slight warmth and tingling remained. He'd never admit it to anyone, but the sensations had him hard and ready to rut against the leather seat.

"No humping your motorbike." Gray flicked him on the back of the neck before continuing toward his Harley. "How long do you think this summer weather will last?"

"Who knows." Scottie rode his old Triumph rain, shine, or snow.

Gray paused with his helmet in his hands. "I heard you used to surf."

"I did."

Sort of.

"Why'd you stop?" Gray prompted. "Scottie?"

Scottie stared down at the helmet clutched in his hands. "Fuck if I know."

In truth, Scottie hadn't really thought much about surfing in ages. After leaving rugby, he'd thrown himself into learning a new sport. He'd started learning in the hopes of it filling his time.

Drinking had been the crutch Scottie turned to instead. In retrospect, it would've been better to stay with surfing. *Even if I am shit at it.* From the pointed look Gray sent him, the man clearly believed he should give it another try.

"Are there even places to surf here?" Gray swung his leg over his Harley and walked it closer to Scottie. "You'll have to teach me."

"How to surf?" Scottie blinked stupidly at him. "You want to surf?"

"Yes."

"Right." Scottie didn't believe it for a second. "Don't do much surfing anymore. Got bored with it."

The real truth about his surfing was Scottie had gotten to the point where he felt idiotic for falling off the board all the time. He hadn't told any of his friends. They'd all assumed he'd done brilliantly at it from how he talked about it.

Giving it another go wasn't high on his priority list. Boxing worked much better at helping him maintain the calm that rehab had brought to him. He had no doubt teaching Gray would be a terrible idea.

"Scottie?" Gray snapped his fingers in front of his face.

"We don't have to surf."

"Boxing is more my thing." Scottie skirted the issue by changing the subject. "Are we going to Ruck or are we sitting on our arses outside your cottage all day like a pair of garden gnomes?"

"Should I leave you tied up to the cross for a few more hours?" Gray's eyes glinted in the midmorning sun. "See if you can keep up with me, boy."

By the time they arrived outside of the restaurant, Scottie had reconsidered the concept of sitting altogether. His arse twinged periodically as a reminder of the morning's adventure. His friends would tease him mercilessly if they even had a hint of his discomfort—and the reason behind it.

His former rugby mates stood outside Ruck chatting when Scottie pulled up on his bike a second after Gray. He parked his bike and pulled off his helmet as a wave of uneasiness struck him over what they'd all assume about him arriving with Gray. He reminded himself that his friends would never begrudge him a healthy relationship.

They'll tease the fuck out of me, but they want me happy.

The words from his therapist came back to him almost immediately. *You've trusted them on the rugby pitch, you can do the same with the sober and saner version of yourself.* Scottie took comfort in the fact that if they disappointed him, he could always kick their arses.

"So? Am I fired?" Gray's blunt question drew Scottie out of his thoughts. "No point in wasting my time if you've already decided."

"Over what?" Remi asked, appearing genuinely confused.

BC and Taine seemed equally befuddled. "Are you talking about the article? Nonsense. They've all been in tabloids as well, more than once. We're not hypocrites."

"Oi. Frenchie." BC punched Remi in the shoulder. "You had your fair share of attention back in the day."

Remi stared dismissively at BC before returning his attention to Gray. "You're not fired."

"Good." Gray held his helmet under his arm and waited a few seconds in the growing silence. "Well, we going inside or are you all waiting for a sign from heaven?"

"Americans." Scottie grinned, and BC laughed in response. "Such rude bastards."

Gray's eyes narrowed on him with a promise of punishment that sent a shiver up Scottie's spine. "Yet, here we are, still hanging around outside waiting for a miracle."

The former marine walked between them toward the door to open Ruck and head inside. It took a bit of playful pushing and shoving before the others made their way inside. It was far easier for Scottie to see the genuine camaraderie between himself and his friends without the haze of alcohol and anger blinding him to it.

Allowing the others to head toward the largest table in the dining room, Scottie held back to centre himself. The epiphany had hit him out of nowhere. All this time, he'd been angry at never having a family, but he'd had one all along from the friends he'd met through rugby.

I'm a moron.

These bastards have been here for me through all my shit, and I never bothered to see it.

"Oi. Monk. Get your arse over here." Caddock whistled loudly for him. "Your old man promised to cook us up a sample of the menus for the next month. It's the only damn reason I make the trip out here every few weeks. You know how far it is from Looe? It takes forever."

"It's a three-hour drive. Stop acting like you're going to the moon and back." Remi, ever the realist, shut down the whining from Caddock and BC, who'd started to chime in with his own complaints. "Does your American need any help?"

"My American?" Scottie repeated. He decided maybe disappearing into the kitchen might be a great idea. "I'll go see if he wants a hand."

"No hand jobs in the kitchen," BC yelled after him, sending his friends into fits of laughter.

Scottie flipped them all off with both hands—just for emphasis. "Go fuck yourselves."

CHAPTER SIXTEEN

GRAY

"Gray? You in here?"

Gray leaned his head out of the walk-in freezer to find Wyatt and Hamish standing awkwardly in the kitchen with Yara hovering beside them. "One second."

Tossing the additional ingredients into the tray in his hand, Gray carried it out to set it on one of the work tables. He gestured to one of his current batch of culinary students to get them to begin prepping the food. Yara waved cheerfully at him then disappeared out into the dining area once it became clear the two strangers weren't unwanted intruders.

"I haven't seen you two idiots in a while. Did you get lost on your way to work this morning?" Gray motioned for them to follow him down the hall toward his office. "If it's about the trash in the paper, I've decided to ignore it."

Hamish waited until they'd all gotten seated in the privacy of the office to speak. "Have we ever given a shit about your personal life?"

"Yes." Gray stared pointedly at both of them until they had the decency to flush. He could distinctly recall one occasion many years ago when the two men had tried too hard to dig into his personal life. "You paid for it."

"We're not here to drag up ancient history." Wyatt rubbed the back of his neck and shifted uncomfortably. "Shit. How do you still manage to make me feel like a recruit straight out of boot camp."

"Practice." Gray leaned back in his seat and took a closer look at his old friends. They appeared tired and worried from their tense shoulders and the bags under their eyes. "What's going on?"

"We lost Vinnie and Lily." Hamish shifted forward to rest his elbows on his knees.

"Lost them how?" Gray had a distinct feeling they hadn't gotten the direction wrong on the way to Ruck.

"We lost Vinnie first. Lily went after him." Wyatt paused to glare sharply at Hamish. "She didn't believe we were taking it seriously."

"Were you taking it seriously?" Gray asked pointedly.

Silence is never good.

"So, no then?" Gray raised his eyebrows at the two men. "All right, look, you're both acting like pimply teenagers who've been called to the principal's office. You obviously want my help. Get to the point of the story or get the fuck out. I'm busy. And if you hadn't noticed, I've retired from the 'jumping in to save the day' business."

Hamish exchanged a look at Wyatt before obviously reaching a decision. "Vinnie went off to the Philippines to help a friend who went missing while hiking. He took time off to do it. It wasn't a contract for us. We hadn't heard from him in a few days when Lily asked if we shouldn't at least ask the authorities to check on him. We said to wait. She hopped on a plane."

"Now they've both disappeared on us. Not answering their phones. Nye's tracked them to a particular island, but that doesn't help us all the way over here." Wyatt picked up the story. "You're the best tracker that I've ever met in all my years of military service."

"Fancy a trip with us?" Hamish asked.

Leaning even further back in his chair, Gray stared up at the ceiling while considering. He had experience in tracking in a tropical environment. As far as he could see, only one important detail stood in his way—the restaurant couldn't run itself.

The culinary students worked hard, but he didn't trust them to handle however long it would take to find Vinnie and Lily. Gray finally tilted forward to face his old military friends. They'd waited patiently for him to think it over.

"I can't just leave Ruck." Gray held up his hand to stop Hamish from responding. "Give me a few hours to talk it over and see if I can find a temporary replacement. Book a flight for me."

"Just you?"

"You think three of us won't stand out in the Philippines?

If you want this under the radar, it's better for my old retired self to go in on my own. They'll probably assume I'm reliving my glory days or some stupid shit." Gray dug into his pocket to find his phone to text Scottie about his change of plans. "Hamster. Does your baker know any local chefs?"

"I'll ask." Hamish grabbed his own phone and stepped out of the office to make a call.

"Gray?"

"Yeah?" He looked up to find Wyatt looking more pensive than normal. "Don't break your brain thinking, Earp. Aled won't thank me."

"Don't be a douche canoe. I'm just trying to say thanks." Wyatt nodded towards the door that Hamish had closed. "He's worried. You know how he gets about those under his command."

"I've seen the tattoo. Hell, I know some of the names on his back." Gray knew first-hand how much it hurt to lose a fellow marine. "And don't act like you're not just as worried. I don't buy your macho SEAL shit any more than I did when you tried it when you were fresh out of selection."

"Asshole."

"Did I poke a hole in your ego again?" Gray smirked at the former SEAL, who bristled almost instinctively. "Do me a favour?"

"No." Wyatt glared at him. "Fine. What?"

"Keep an eye on Alice and Alex." Gray found himself worrying about the twins as if they were his own kids most of the time. He still hadn't figured out how they'd wormed their way into his life like they had. "They usually have breakfast with me a couple times a week."

Hamish poked his head back into the office, disrupting whatever Wyatt had been about to say. "Nye's booking a flight for you. Aled has a friend who's in the process of building her restaurant. She could easily fill in for you for a week."

Gray pinched the bridge of his nose and took a few deep breaths before making his decision. "Fine. Let me know when I'm flying out. I'll need to figure out how to get some gear into the country with me."

"Thank you." Hamish stepped back out of the room with his phone still pressed to his ear. "We'll see if we can get someone to meet you in Manila."

Gray levelled a glare at Wyatt. "You both owe me."

"Damn it."

After Wyatt and Hamish both left to handle the arrangements, Gray took a few minutes to jot down notes on the menu plans, inventory, and deliveries for the next two weeks at Ruck. His impromptu vacation shouldn't require more than a few days, but it never hurt to be excessively prepared. Experience taught him not to expect the worst without evidence while preparing for it anyway.

"Don't hover, kitten." Gray didn't look up from the notes he was jotting down. He'd heard footsteps in the hall and correctly assumed it was Scottie. "I'll be gone for a few days. Behave yourself."

Scottie bristled as Gray had expected. "Don't catch anything contagious."

Gray gathered up his papers, smirking at the man standing uneasily by the door. "Why don't you follow me home, kitten? We can say our goodbyes. Earp's giving me a ride to the airport, but I want my bike secured in the garage."

"Who says I want to say goodbye? I've got shit to do." Scottie crossed his arms only to unfold them to reach out to take the papers that Gray held out to him. "What's this, then?"

"Make sure whoever comes in to temporarily take over the restaurant gets those." Gray watched him for a few seconds, noticing his tense shoulders and the tightening of his jaw. "Behave yourself, kitten."

"Fuck off."

Gray walked around the desk and reached down to grasp Scottie through his jeans. "Keep your hands off *my* property."

"Or?"

"It'll be longer than a few minutes before you can sit on your ass." Gray winked at him and gave one last squeeze. "Good boy."

Thoughts of Scottie made the long flight easier to suffer through. Gray had never been a fan of being stuck on a plane for any length of time. He even managed to sleep through most of the trip.

Gray: Landed safely. Met your contact. Heading out.

Wyatt: You do know text messaging isn't morse code. You can use complete sentences.

Gray: Fuck. Off.

Wyatt: Yeah, yeah, old man. Keep your dentures in.

Gray: You keep on with the jokes while I track down your lost sheep.

Wyatt: Aled said to tell you the twins said hi. They apparently had breakfast with Scottie this morning. Did you drop him on his head?

Gray: Turning my phone off now.

CHAPTER SEVENTEEN

SCOTTIE

Three days into Gray's absence, Scottie found himself sitting at a table in the bar portion of the Sin Bin. Several of his friends were in town and had come together to celebrate Remi and Sarah's wedding anniversary. His brother had joined them as well, only to disappear a few minutes into arriving with Zeb Chardin to go dancing.

French bastard.

Bottles and glasses of various alcoholic beverages littered the table. Scottie had thus far ignored the lot of them, drinking a soda instead. He itched to grab one or seven; anything to wash away the uneasiness that had settled in his gut not long after Gray had left.

"You don't want that." Remi's hand dropped on his arm

to block Scottie when he reached for a bottle. "Why don't we have them clear the table?"

"The fuck I don't." Scottie scowled at Remi, who merely glared right back at him. He eventually released the bottle with a resigned sigh. "Thanks, Frenchie."

Waving off the offer to clear the table, Scottie reminded himself why he'd agreed to come to the club. He didn't want his life to change just because he'd stopped drinking. The temptation to grab one of the beers disappeared the more he thought about why rehab had been necessary to begin with.

"My cousin is young and arrogant." Remi drew Scottie out of his thoughts. The Frenchman had clearly decided his scowl was directed at the younger men who'd just walked across the room past their table. "But he's not prone to breaking hearts or using men if that is your concern."

Scottie's eyes narrowed further on Remi. He'd been trying to keep his mind away from Zeb and didn't want the reminder. "He's a punk."

"I believe the phrase is 'it takes one to know one.'" Remi easily blocked the half-hearted swat Scottie aimed at his arm. "How's your American doing?"

"Not mine," he muttered unconvincingly.

"Oui." Remi saluted him with his glass of wine. "Yes. It seems you are more his than he is yours. Are you confident the lifestyle is one you're truly ready to submerse yourself into?"

His first instinct was to tell Remi to mind his own business, with a few expletives to add emphasis. Scottie bit back the words, drinking a quarter of his soda to swallow down his anger. He spluttered through the fizzing in the back of his throat, ignoring the amused laughter coming from the man sitting next to him.

Of all his friends, Remi and Taine both had experience in the BDSM and fetish world. The Frenchie probably had the most out of the two. Scottie could likely ask him anything, but he'd never been one to share everything, even with his friends.

"It doesn't make you weak." Remi cut the silence with a sharp comment that hit to the heart of his greatest internalised fear. "Sarah would say she retains all of the power in our relationship. It takes a strong woman or man to submit to another. My control comes from doing everything I can to satisfy her needs, even the ones she doesn't yet know she has."

"How fucking fascinating," Scottie said dismissively, though he didn't quite mean it.

"Do you miss your American?" Remi appeared completely determined to slice away at all of the walls that Scottie had thrown up around himself. "Some submissives can frequently feel the absence of their lover more than others in a less intense relationship."

The two men had been speaking quietly, allowing the ambient noise of the bar to drown out the conversation. Scottie clammed up instantly when Taine scooted closer to them. He trusted all of his friends, but not with his more vulnerable side.

Despite the numerous lengthy talks with Gray prior to getting involved, Scottie hadn't expected the man's absence to throw him. Remi continued to stare at him until he flipped Frenchie off. They returned their attention to the rest of the group.

Heart to heart time is over.

Deciding he'd had enough, Scottie said his goodbyes and headed out of the Sin Bin. Without drinking, he didn't enjoy the nightclub quite as much. *Or maybe I just miss Gray.*

The entire way to his flat, Scottie couldn't quite shake his need to speak with Gray. He had no idea what the time difference was between Cardiff and wherever the man had gone. Trying to talk himself out of texting him seemed a mission doomed to failure—until he arrived home to find his father slumped on the steps leading up to the building.

Ahh, fuck.

Stowing his bike in his parking space, Scottie quickly strode down the walk and up the few steps to his father. He crouched down to ensure his old man hadn't died. *Trust the bastard to drag his drunken arse to my house.*

He hadn't died.

More's the pity.

I could just leave the fucker on the steps.

Up close and personal, Scottie easily smelled the booze on him. It made his stomach turn—the sour stench of stale beer and body odour. He suddenly found himself grateful for Remi's intervention at the club.

I never want to be this—to be him.

Ever again.

CHAPTER EIGHTEEN

GRAY

Why the fuck did I agree to traipse across the ocean to the tropics in August when it's hotter than a jalapeno's armpit?

Despite Hamish and Wyatt's obvious concern, Gray couldn't convince himself that the missing idiots had actually gotten into danger. They were smart—capable. Neither prone to allowing themselves to be drawn into a situation they couldn't escape from.

Before spending time as a drill instructor, Gray spent a lot of time teaching both tracking and SERE tactics to Marine snipers, SEALs, and Rangers. He was one of the best, which was likely why Wyatt had come to him instead of handling it himself.

I'm dripping with sweat.

I'm old.

I'm tired.

These fuckers better be in dire straits, or I'm kicking their arses all the way back to Cardiff.

Following a trail of sightings by locals, Gray eventually wound up in a remote village on the island of Leyte, which had recently suffered a catastrophic landslide. He found Vinnie and Lily helping a missionary. They seemed genuinely surprised and perturbed to see him.

"I told those wankers that I'd be out of contact. First they send Lily, and now you." Vinnie stepped away to converse with Gray after the missionary frowned at him for his language. "What the bloody hell did they think might happen to me on vacation? It's not like I was gone for months."

"Wait. What? They told me Lily was worried." Gray made a mental note to kick the two men's arses the moment he arrived back in Wales. "Why exactly did they send me here?"

Lily wandered over to join them. "I came to help Vinnie with the volunteer work."

"I'm clearly missing something here." Gray frowned at both of them. "Did you lie to them or are they lying to me?"

No response, which is answer enough, I suppose.

"Why didn't you text them?" Gray crossed his arms while maintaining a tight control on his anger to avoid exploding on the two of them. "It would've taken a second to text or email them to allay their genuine concerns for your health. Hamish has lost several Royal Marines under his command; of course he's going to worry. So, again I ask, why the fuck didn't you contact them?"

Lily shifted on her feet with obvious unease. "Sorry?"

Gray snorted, partly amused but mostly still annoyed. "You're usually a much better liar."

Vinnie sidled up next to Lily and threw his arm around her shoulder, grunting when she elbowed him hard in the side. "*Oi.* Look, ever since the bombing at the hospital in Syria while we were working with the doctors, Hamish, in particular, treats us like death is just around the corner and we're too young to realise it. We're not children."

"You're sulking in the Philippines." Gray scratched at his beard for a few seconds. "Why not sit them down and have a conversation if you're such mature grown-ups?"

"Dunno," Vinnie shrugged. "I wanted some fresh air to escape the claustrophobic feeling in the office."

"Fucking children." Gray pinched the bridge of his nose and restrained his sudden urge to knock their heads together repeatedly. "Call them. Or text them. *Now.* I'm going home. I am too old for this idiotic horseshit."

"Want to help us with rebuilding some of the houses for a few days?" Lily asked.

Glancing around at the ruined houses, mud-covered streets, and the haunted eyes of many of the people, Gray caved to the inevitable. He decided to stay on the condition Vinnie immediately reach out to Wyatt and Hamish. With the prodigal children apologising, he walked away to find some privacy to have a quick text conversation with Scottie.

Gray: Think I'll be here for a few more days.

Scottie: It's two in the morning.

Gray: Miss me?

Scottie: Fuck off. I'm trying to sleep.

Gray: Are you itching for a spanking, kitten?

Gray: Hands off your dick. I'm assuming that's why it's been several minutes.

Scottie: Going to sleep. Hope you trip over a coconut and bash your head in.

Gray: Pleasant dreams, kitten.

I am a sadistic son of a gun.

Gray enjoyed the thrill of teasing a submissive. Always had. His mind had already started to ponder the numerous ways to sensually torment Scottie when he finally got back to Cardiff. *Oh, that arse is going to be pink again.*

"Oi. Gray."

He shoved his phone into his pocket and waved Lily over. "What?"

"The Hamster is bringing everyone over to help in the village." Lily hopped up onto a nearby wall. "He said they'd book a return flight for you whenever you're ready to go. We don't want you to have to miss too many days at Ruck."

"Guilty conscience messing with you?"

"Nah." She shrugged. "They said we—"

"Do I look like your counsellor or your chaplain? You want to feel less guilty, make it right with Wyatt and Hamish. Leave me the fuck out of it." Gray had no desire to insert himself any further into the useless dramatics. He really had better things to do with his time. "Where are they putting the volunteers up for the night? My old bones have spent hours on a plane and even more trying to find you idiotic maggots. I'm going to need a damn nap."

"We are sorry, you know?" Lily grinned when he sighed

deeply at her. "Missing your boy toy?"

"Submissives miss me," Gray stated baldly.

Lily flushed before her smile widened further. "Do you spank him?"

"I believe that's none of your goddamn business." Gray found his tolerance for the younger Brits who worked with his old friends quickly evaporating.

"So, that's a yes." Lily laughed before he knocked her off the wall with an unexpected shove. "*Oi.*"

"Children."

CHAPTER NINETEEN

SCOTTIE

"Why does he have to stay another week?" Scottie had been whinging about it for the past hour, even though he firmly claimed not to be sulking or pouting—at all. He glared at Silus when he snickered. "Don't be an arse."

With his university term starting in a couple of weeks, Silus had finally decided to finish getting his flat situated. Scottie had managed to see him a couple of times since his brother had moved. Today he'd brought over a pizza to help him put some shelves together.

"Just admit you miss your American." Silus lifted his head up from where he'd been hunting for a missing part. "Are you sure we need the bolt?"

"If you want your books to stay on the shelves, yes, you do. If you're not fussed, then see what happens without it."

Scottie felt almost parental, showing his younger brother how to build a bookcase. "And I'll admit nothing to your nosy arse."

"Success!" Silus held up the tiny bolt with a triumphant grin. "My nose is on my face where it belongs."

Rolling his eyes at his snickering brother, Scottie grabbed the bolt to secure the last of the shelves. They'd worked on the bookcases for several hours already. The time had flown by as the half-siblings enjoyed each other's company.

With the last shelf done, Scottie used brute force to manoeuvre the heavy shelf into place against the wall. He brushed his hands off on his jeans and happily accepted the cold bottle of water from Silus. They collapsed onto the tiny sofa—crushed together on the tiny thing to watch the ending of the football match on Silus's small telly.

"I'm buying you a bigger telly." Scottie thought the screen was only slightly bigger than a laptop's. "And an adult-sized couch."

"It is adult-sized. Not all adults are the equivalent of an overgrown yeti. Plus, I'm a university student." Silus waved off his offer dismissively. "I'm not going to live in the lap of luxury."

"Fine. Keep your toy sofa and your duct-taped car." Scottie shifted around on the couch, almost knocking Silus off it in the process. "What if Santa brings you one for Christmas?"

"It's barely September. You'll have forgotten about this by December." Silus grabbed his mobile when it started to ring with a tune that sounded familiar to Scottie. "Zeb? Can I call you back?"

At the familiar name, Scottie's eyes narrowed on Silus, who made the wise decision to finish his conversation in the bedroom. *Why the fuck is that French shit calling my little brother?* He told himself it wasn't his business, and the young Chardin hadn't done anything to truly earn his ire.

Still a little shit.

Before Silus returned to the room, Scottie's mobile buzzed in his pocket to alert him to a text message. *Ahh, Gray.* The brief note told him that the American would be returning to Cardiff at the end of the week. Despite all his efforts, he couldn't quite wipe the grin off his face.

"Hear from your sugar daddy?"

Scottie grabbed the nearest object, a pair of socks, and beamed them at his brother. "I probably have more money than he does."

Silus caught the socks, sniffed them, and tossed them into a nearby basket. "Clean."

"What did the—"

Silus held up a hand to stop him mid-sentence. "His name is Zeb. I have no idea why you're such a jerk whenever he's mentioned. He's brilliant."

"Fuck," Scottie groaned, sinking further into the couch. "Am I going to have to play nice with Zippie?"

"Yes."

"Fine." He glared at his brother who grinned at him.

"Not going to argue?" Silus grabbed the box of pizza from the table and held it out to him. "I figured you'd have a six-page summary of why I should stay away from him."

"You're a Monk." Scottie had never met a member of his

family who wasn't stubborn. "I'd be wasting my breath. Plus, if he breaks your heart, I'll have a legitimate reason to beat the shit out of him that even Remi can't argue with."

"Well, at least you have a goal in mind." Silus grabbed a slice of pizza from the box and sat cross-legged on the floor. "Try to be nice to him."

"Shit," Scottie grumbled around his mouthful of food. He wanted to argue with his little brother but knew it would be pointless. "Have any plans for the evening?"

"None of your business." Silus became very interested in the slice of pizza in his hand.

"Where's Zippie taking you?" he asked with a knowing grin. "Fucker better treat you right, or I'll kick his arse back across the channel."

"You wouldn't, it's too much work." His brother leaned to the right to avoid the second pair of socks. "Stop tossing my clean laundry everywhere."

"Why are your socks all over the couch?" Scottie had found bits and pieces of his brother's laundry scattered around the flat. "Actually, never mind, you might break my brain."

"Don't want to risk what's left after playing rugby?" Silus snickered—again.

"Oi. You cheeky little fucker." Scottie leapt up from the couch and caught his foot on the coffee table squashed right up next to it. He fell forward like a log, crashing through the wood and landing on his stomach amidst the wreckage of his brother's cheap furniture. "Well, shit."

"My table."

"Your table?" Scottie carefully got to his feet while

brushing debris off his jeans. "Well, you sure you don't want me to buy you some new furniture?"

"Fine. Let's go to Ikea." Silus grabbed his car keys, stared down at them, and then glared at Scottie. "If you ruin my car so you can buy me a new one, I'm hacking your mobile to send naked pictures to everyone in your contact list."

"Wouldn't be the first time." Scottie kicked at the ruined coffee table. "Why don't I get my friend who works in waste management to drive out to get your couch, coffee table, and bed? I'll buy you a whole new set of furniture. And I promise to leave your piece of shit car alone."

"*Fine.*"

"Stubborn arse." He winked at Silus, who flipped him off. "Can you hack anyone's phone?"

"No."

"But—"

"No, I'm not hacking any of your friends' mobiles so you can prank them." Silus herded Scottie out of the small flat. "You're an idiot, but I love you."

CHAPTER TWENTY

GRAY

Flying from Cebu to London to Cardiff, Gray made his way out of the airport with the sole desire to find his own bed in his own home and sleep for a few days. He hadn't expected to find anyone waiting for him by the exit. Scottie looked both sheepish and angry at himself.

"I didn't miss you." Scottie grabbed the bag from him and headed out of the airport with Gray trailing after him. "And you can stop laughing at me right now."

Chuckling even more at the grumbling, Gray followed him to the car park. They stopped at a shiny new Jaguar SUV. Scottie tossed his bag into the back of the vehicle and turned toward him.

"New vehicle?"

"Slight issue with my bike." Scottie's mood seemed to

darken almost immediately.

"Oh?" Gray hadn't heard anything from either the twins or anyone else about Scottie getting in an accident. "What issue?"

"My old man drove over it while trying to park outside of my flat." His lover shook his arms as if attempting to release his anger. "Or so he claims. I think the fucker was angry I wouldn't give him any money for liquor. I said I'd pay for his treatment to keep the bastard alive. He's more interested in drinking himself into the grave faster."

Gray brought his hands up to rest on Scottie's tense shoulders. He massaged them firmly while meeting his gaze. "Proud of you for making the offer to help him, kitten. It takes a strong man to offer kindness to someone who abused them."

"I'm an idiot." Scottie snorted derisively.

"No, you're hurting." Gray shifted one of his hands to grip his submissive by the back of the neck firmly. He peered over his shoulder into the vehicle. "Looks spacious."

Scottie leaned back into the hand on his neck. "It is."

All the exhaustion from his trip suddenly evaporated, Gray dug into Scottie's pockets to find the keys to the Jaguar. He had plans for their drive back to his cottage, ones that required him to be in control of the vehicle. To his surprise, Scottie didn't argue with him.

"I didn't miss you," Scottie repeated absently after several minutes of silence.

"So you've said, kitten." Gray stretched his arm across the centre console and dropped it directly on Scottie's crotch. "I punish lies, boy. Is that what you want? Do you need a session on the cross? Or maybe something more?"

"I didn't…." Scottie trailed off when Gray squeezed his cock hard. "I might've missed you."

Gray tightened his hold.

"I missed you, sir."

"Good boy." He continued his firm massage of Scottie's shaft through his jeans. "There's a private club in Cardiff that caters to gay Dominants. It's run by a couple who I've known for a while. They moved up from London three years ago to open the Red Card."

"I'd be front page news in the morning." Scottie shook his head, though from the twitching of the cock in Gray's hand, he was at least a little interested. "And you can't make me go."

Gray lifted his hand away from Scottie. They both needed clear heads to discuss boundaries. "If you truly aren't interested, I would never betray your trust by forcing you into it. What if I could guarantee no one would see your face or your tattoos? A little exhibition and vulnerability within a controlled environment. Risk without actual risk."

"Is that even possible?"

"Leo and Dimas run a nightclub. They pride themselves on the exclusivity and privacy of the Red Card. It's usually frequented by people who have something to lose if their chosen lifestyle were to be front page news." Gray had known Leolin Priddy for many years. They'd met at a BDSM club in New York City; they shared similar tastes in submissives. Leo was one of the few Dominants that he considered to be a friend. "You might enjoy talking to Dimas Acosta."

"The footballer?" Scottie sat up in the chair. "Are you kidding me? He's a submissive."

Gray sent a bemused smile at him. "Scottie Monk is a submissive. Why couldn't a famous soccer player be one as well?"

"Football, not soccer," Scottie corrected. "How private is the club?"

"Only card-carrying members are allowed inside. The club provides masks to completely cover the faces of both Dominants and submissives. All members are required to sign non-disclosure agreements. It's fucking expensive to join as well." Gray only knew about Dimas because he'd had dinner with the couple a few times since moving to Cardiff. "What do you think, kitten? Are you interested?"

Scottie reached down to adjust himself in his trousers, shifting in the seat. "Fuck."

That's a yes.

"Use your words, boy." Gray refused to move forward on the idea forming in his mind unless Scottie gave a confident answer. He firmly believed submissives had to decide to cross lines on their own. "Well?"

"Yes."

Gray reached his hand out to resume his fondling of Scottie's cock through his jeans. "How many times do you have to be told to ask nicely?"

Scottie glared at him but bucked up against Gray's hand. "I want to go to the bloody club."

Gray remained silent.

Scottie huffed in annoyance at the silence, and finally

asked with a hint of anger in his voice, "Will you take me to the club, sir?"

"Would you like me to parade you around as mine?" Gray slowly lowered Scottie's zipper and worked his hand inside. "Show you off to all the other Dominants? Pinken your ass while you're tied up in front of everyone?"

"Yes." Scottie inhaled sharply when Gray's hand made it inside his boxers to wrap around his cock. "Yes. *Please.*"

"Can you imagine yourself bound before a cheering audience who has no idea who you are?" Gray described in graphic detail what he had planned while continuing to stroke his Scottie's cock. "You'd beg for it, wouldn't you? Like a good kitten."

With most of his attention on not wrecking the new Jaguar, Gray drove Scottie to the brink with his words and his fingers. Though their separation hadn't been for an extended period, they'd both felt the absence. The climax took both men by surprise.

"You did miss me." Gray smirked while pulling his hand free, covered in the evidence of Scottie's orgasm. He held his fingers up to the younger man's lips. "Lick them clean. And kitten?"

"What?" Scottie managed to appear turned on and ticked off at the same time.

"I'm happy to see you too."

CHAPTER TWENTY-ONE

SCOTTIE

Despite his "yes," it was two weeks into September before Scottie managed to talk himself into approaching Gray about a date to the Red Card. He'd ignored the idea for a while. It took another run-in with his father to tip him over the edge.

For the third time in a month, his old man had shown up at Scottie's flat drunk, incoherent, and belligerent. He wanted to slam the door in his father's face but didn't. Silus's admonishment to treat him with kindness stopped him.

Father and son had screamed at each other until the drunken bastard passed out cold on the sofa. Scottie waited until morning to bundle his dad into his vehicle and drive him back to his own home. He dumped him on his bed and left without saying another word.

I'm done.

I can't do this week after week.

Fuck this guilt I feel.

I don't owe him a bloody thing.

He'd grabbed his mobile to send a text the second he'd gotten back into his Jaguar.

Scottie: You up for a visit to the Red Card?

Gray: Are you texting because you can't say the words out loud?

Gray: Meet me at Ruck at closing.

That's it? Just meet me?

Cryptic American bastard.

Scottie drove up in his Jaguar outside of Ruck in time to see Silus and Zeb walking down the pavement toward the Sin Bin. "You little French bastard."

Thankfully for all of them, neither Zeb nor Silus heard him. Scottie forced himself to count to ten several times. It always amazed him how his coping skills from rehab worked in all aspects of his life. He watched his younger brother disappear into the club with a resigned sigh.

"Leave the youngsters alone, kitten." Gray stepped up to the vehicle and rested his arms against the door, hands dangling through the open window. "Dimas and Leo have a private room set up for us to get changed when we arrive."

"Changed?" Scottie frowned at Gray, who ignored him to climb into the SUV. "What do you mean, changed?"

"Patience, boy."

With a lot of grumbling, Scottie pulled away from the kerb to drive across Cardiff to the club. He was surprised when Gray didn't touch him. *Trying to drive me crazy.*

Parking in the reserved spot in the back of a plain, nondescript brick building, Scottie allowed himself to be led to the red door of the club. The muscled bouncer glanced at them before directing them inside. He couldn't help the slight shiver up his spine while they made their way through the darkened hallway past a series of rooms before entering one on the left that had a nameplate with *Gandalf* on it.

"What's with the name?" Scottie glanced around the sparsely decorated room that felt more like a castle dungeon. "This is some medieval shit."

"Leo has a sense of humour." Gray gestured toward two sets of clothing hanging from wrought iron racks on the faux stone wall. "You'll find the one on the right is yours."

On closer inspection, Scottie thought clothing might be a stretch for the items designated for him. He picked up a full leather body harness that attached to a jockstrap, with a sense of trepidation. *I'm going to freeze my balls off in this and how the hell is this going to keep my identity a secret?*

"The club keeps the heat on to ensure both the participants and the voyeurs are comfortable in whatever their state." Gray waved a piece of what appeared to be parchment paper at him. "They also provide various styles of masks, which are required wearing. I'm leaning toward the puppy mask."

"Fuck off." Scottie narrowed his eyes on the smirking American while he stripped out of his clothes. "Not your bitch."

"Careful, kitten." Gray set the paper aside and retrieved a large box from the nearby settee. "I picked masks for both of us."

Scottie forced himself to look inside, only to feel immediately relieved. "Reminds me of something from *Casanova*."

Gray lifted out a black-and-gold mask, holding it up to Scottie's face and carefully securing it with thin straps. It covered his face completely with the elongated nose and sharply pointed jawline going past his chin. "I think this design is called a Bauta. Tie mine on?"

All of their clothes, wallets, and watches went into a safe in the corner. Gray set up the code to lock it, winking at Scottie who felt completely naked in his outfit. *Hell. I am fucking nude as can be.* He appreciated the way the leather trousers accentuated Gray's lower half.

"I feel like an idiot." Scottie stood in front of a full-length mirror checking himself out. The leather jockstrap barely covered his shaft that Gray had already slipped a ring onto. His leather harness rubbed against his nipples whenever he shifted even a little. "What the hell am I doing?"

Gray dropped a hand possessively on Scottie's bare arse and squeezed each cheek. "You ready? Not too late to back out."

"As you were." Scottie heard more confidence in his voice than he felt. "Why do you get actual leather trousers and my arse is hanging out for all to see?"

Gray slid a finger along the cleft of Scottie's behind. "No more talking, kitten. I wouldn't want to jump straight to punishment."

Biting his lip to keep a moan from escaping, Scottie told himself that it was no different from walking onto a rugby pitch. *Naked. That's one big-arse difference.* The hand on him distracted him nicely from the sudden attack of nerves.

After attaching a lead to the ring at the base of Scottie's throat that made up part of the harness, Gray guided him out of their private room. They strode down the dimly lit hallway until reaching what the brochure referred to as the appetiser. It was a section meant for casual dancing and drinks, likely meant to put newcomers at ease.

The waiters were as scantily clad as Scottie. Gray ordered for them both. Scottie remembered almost too late not to speak; a hard tug on the leash let him know his slip had been caught.

Punishment.

I like punishment a bit too much.

It was a truth Scottie hadn't admitted to Gray. From the bemused smirk, the man already knew it. He had an annoying habit of being able to read his sub's mind.

"Let's get comfortable." Gray found a small table with a single leather armchair in one of the dark corners near the bar. He used his foot to nudge a cushion out from under the table. "Sit, boy."

Scottie stared from the cushion to Gray who simply drew the leash down to force him to kneel on it. "Bastard."

"Do I need to check fire or are you simply hoping a second infraction will mean a harsher punishment?" Gray motioned for the waiter to set their drinks on the table. His attention stayed on Scottie. "You are eager for my attention, aren't you? Good boy."

Fuck.

Knowing Gray expected an answer, Scottie could only nod

in response. He didn't understand the part of him that thrived in the role of submissive, but he also couldn't deny it either. The connection with his Dominant brought depth to their relationship that he'd never experienced before.

"Gandalf the Gray."

"I'd kick your ass if I didn't appreciate your generosity." Gray stood up to shake the hand of an impeccably dressed man in a silver mask, who had a submissive kneeling at his side. "Why don't you two come by Ruck next week so I can return the favour? You can meet my kitten officially."

"I'll text you. Enjoy your evening. We've set up the Andrew's room for you. When you finish your drinks, head down the hall to the Main Course. You'll find one of the doors has a red cross on it. That's the one you want." The man nodded to Gray, smirked down at Scottie, and then wandered off with his partner crawling slowly behind him. "We'll be sure to watch the show."

"He's a good Dominant. Overdramatic, but so is his submissive," Gray commented absently. "Come here, boy."

Shifting forward on his knees, Scottie had only inched forward slightly when Gray grabbed his head to shove him into his crotch. A hard shaft poked out of the opening on the American's leather trousers to rub across his mouth. He knew exactly what his appetiser would be.

Gray adjusted himself slightly in the armchair, holding Scottie's head in place. "Use your tongue, kitten."

Kittens like cream.

It took immense effort not to laugh at his own idiotic joke. The hard shaft driving deep into his mouth helped a great deal.

Scottie's own cock tried to twitch with interest, but the ring allowed him only the tease of pleasure.

His body hummed with the thrill of being only partially hidden by the shadows. Scottie had his lips wrapped around his Dominant's cock in plain view of an entire room of men. He sucked harder, took Gray deeper, driven by an exhibitionist urge he didn't know existed in him.

This will be a good night.

Gray pressed Scottie's head down while bucking up into his mouth. "Be a good boy and swallow."

A very good night.

CHAPTER TWENTY-TWO

GRAY

"You touch him again, and I'll break every bone in your hand." Gray had easily stopped the man who grabbed Scottie's arse when they'd walked past him in the hallway. "You never touch anyone without their permission. Ever. And I don't mean their Dominant's permission, either. You don't touch a submissive without their saying yes. Why the hell are you in a bondage club if you can't even understand the basics? *Fuckstick.*"

"I agree." Leo joined them with a bouncer on either side of him. "He won't be back."

Leaving the club owner and employees to handle the situation, Gray continued down the hall toward the Main Course. Scottie's arse on display drew him in like a bear to honey. He had to make his mark on his submissive before the night ended.

First, though, Gray wanted to check in with Scottie—and calm down. He preferred a clear head when planning more complex play. It was also why their drinks all evening had been non-alcoholic.

"Check fire." Gray eased Scottie into an alcove off to the side. "You all right?"

"Fine." Scottie glared over his shoulder toward where the misbehaving man had been dragged off. "I'd like to kick his arse."

"Thanks for trusting me to handle him. It took strength not to break his balls when he grabbed you." Gray had actually expected Scottie to tackle the man and pummel him to the ground. "Do you want to continue or are you done with being exposed for the evening?"

It would be disappointing if their night ended so soon, but understandable. Gray waited while Scottie thought it over. He tried to keep his hands and his eyes off his submissive to avoid temptation.

"As you were."

"Good boy." Gray decided to continue on with his original plan. *Sometimes punishment is the best reward.* "Time to strap you up to the cross."

The Main Course was broken up into a series of individual rooms that had large picture windows. *A voyeur's paradise.* Gray fully intended to enjoy having his submissive on display. He guided them straight to the door with the red cross on it.

Stark black paint covered the walls inside, contrasting against a lush red sofa and burgundy floor. A tall wooden chest on their right stood open to reveal an array of toys, spanking implements, and other necessities for play. He knew from previous visits that everything in the room was sterilised after each use, including the furniture.

Safety first.

Hooking his finger into the ring at the base of Scottie's throat, Gray dragged him close enough to capture his lips in a kiss. His other hand strayed over his sub's exposed skin. A low moan from his submissive had Gray drawing back with a smirk.

Time for restraint.

With a practised ease, Gray placed Scottie against the slats of the cross. He spread and secured his arms and then his legs. With his submissive safely secured, his attention turned to perusing the various instruments of pain and pleasure to find the perfect one to begin the session.

Checking first to ensure none of the bindings was too tight, Gray made certain Scottie was still clear to continue. He intended to continue to monitor the situation carefully regardless. A submissive could change their mind in the blink of an eye and a good Dominant, in his opinion, was always prepared to adjust accordingly.

Time for fun.

After placing a ball gag in Scottie's mouth under his mask, Gray left it unstrapped and told him to drop the gag if he wanted to call things to a halt at any point. A quick look over his shoulder showed a small audience already gathered for the show. He resisted the urge to yank the curtains closed.

Focus on your target, Baird, not a bout of jealousy, no matter how unusual it is.

Taking up one of the floggers, Gray grazed the handle of it along Scottie's inner thigh, up one side and down the other. The gentle touches lulled his submissive into slowly relaxing into his restraints. He continued on for several minutes, prolonging their anticipation.

With a deft flick, Gray used the flogger to deliver a few gentle touches to his upper thighs before moving higher. He expertly aimed his hits to avoid any sensitive spots that might cause damage. His first round created a beautiful row of crisscrossed lines along Scottie's arse.

Setting aside the flogger, Gray's attention shifted to the large array of vibrators. He selected a decent-sized plug and slid a condom over it before lubing it up. Scottie moaned as loudly as the gag would allow when the toy was eased slowly into him.

Why rush when slow movements torture him far more?

With a wicked chuckle, Gray flipped the switch on the base of the plug to turn on the vibration. Though slender, the vibrator was long enough to provide almost constant stimulation to just the right spot inside of Scottie. He had no doubt his submissive would beg for release soon enough.

He'll do it so nicely.

Gray stepped up to press his body flush against Scottie's. His hard cock rubbed ruthlessly against the base of the plug. "All those men watching would kill to be in here with you. Big, strong, alpha male submissive, tied up and at their mercy. But they can't, can they? You're fucking mine, kitten. I'm going to make sure that they—and you—have no doubts about it."

Scottie bucked as far as the restraint allowed. The gag

prevented any other response. It became clear quickly that he was attempting to grind himself against Gray's cock.

"Good boy." Gray bit down on his neck, sucking hard to leave a mark. Another reminder. "I'm proud of you, kitten."

For the next twenty minutes, Gray teased and tormented Scottie. He used the flogger and a special paddle that contained both a soft side and a hard leather one, all the while watching his submissive's reactions carefully. In one session, he learned a great deal of how to set up their future play.

Crops were definitely out. Scottie had tensed up immediately and not in a good way. Gray had enough experience with submissives to tell even without verbal cues when something wasn't enjoyable.

The paddle turned out to be a revelation. Scottie's muffled groans and constrained movements bordered on desperate with each alternate hard and soft swat. *Perfection.* Gray made a mental note to ask Leo where to get one for his own collection.

Once Scottie's arse was well and truly pinkened, Gray brought the session to a close. He stroked his fingers along the trembling skin gently to bring him down, easing the plug out and dropping it into a nearby basket reserved for used toys. The floggers, paddle, crop, and gag went into it as well, and he yanked the curtains shut.

Show fucking over.

"Easy, kitten." Gray spoke soothingly to his submissive while releasing him from the restraints. His fingers massaged Scottie's arms and legs to avoid any potential cramping. He grabbed a nearby bottle of water. "Let's get some liquid in you."

Aware that Scottie had to be dying to come, Gray led him from the room. They found one of the viewing booths unoccupied and ducked inside it.

Taking a seat, Gray guided Scottie to stand next to him. He reached inside the jockstrap to release his submissive's cock from the ring. His fingers stroked firmly while they watched the couple through the window.

Ahh, Leo and Dimas. I haven't seen one of their sessions in a long while.

"Come for me, kitten," Gray ordered.

Continuing to voice his encouragement, Gray drove his submissive to completion. Scottie wavered on his feet with the power of his climax. Gray put an arm around his waist to keep him from collapsing.

His experience told him Scottie was teetering into sub drop. He'd already begun to shiver. Wiping his hand clean on the jockstrap, Gray led Scottie quickly through the club and back to their private room.

Once Gray had wiped both of them clean with a damp rag, he wrapped Scottie up in a blanket on the large sofa. *Two blankets, actually, massive bastard.* He'd caught the attention of a waiter to order chocolate, a sandwich tray, and hot tea. They sat in silence for several minutes.

Aftercare was as important as any other aspect of the Dominant-submissive relationship. Scottie slowly came back to himself. He glowered at Gray around the large piece of chocolate in his mouth.

Gray waited until he stopped shivering, and his colour had returned to normal. "The drop of adrenaline and the endorphin rush can be a real fucking pain to deal with."

"Tired." Scottie dropped his head back against the couch. "Mind getting my clothes from the safe?"

"How's your arse?"

"Fuck off."

Gray couldn't help chuckling as he got to his feet to open the safe. "I'm serious. If you're sore, there's a cream for it."

"You can kiss my arse. How about that?" Scottie grabbed his clothes from Gray, checking his pockets when his mobile started to buzz. His face paled for a second time when he looked at it. "Fuck."

Gray paused in changing out of the leather gear to his own trousers and shirt. "Scottie? What's wrong?"

"Silus rushed my dad to the hospital." Scottie dropped his phone on the couch and rubbed his eyes roughly with his fingers. "Fuck."

"Easy, kitten." Gray dressed quickly, knowing they'd be going to the hospital. "Get your clothes on. I'll drive while you do some of that weird-ass breathing they taught you."

"*Gray.*"

He knelt in front of Scottie with his hands resting on his knees. "Can't tell you it's going to be all right. He's dying. He was a fucking bastard to you, but it won't make it easier."

"Great pep talk. Did you learn that in the Marines?" Scottie set the cup of tea aside with a preciseness that made Gray wonder if he'd actually wanted to fling it against the wall. "What am I going to do?"

"Get dressed. Go to the hospital. Be there for your brother who is probably as confused as you are." Gray had no doubt

Silus was tearing himself up inside. The youngster didn't have the hard edge that Scottie had built up over the years. "And I'll be here to make sure you don't fall apart."

"Why?" Scottie stared suspiciously at him.

"This? Between us? It's not a once-in-a-while getting a good fuck. It's a relationship. Maybe it's not one others understand, but it's just as deep as any other romance." Gray squeezed his hands around Scottie's knees. "You sure you don't want some cream? Hospital chairs are hard as hell."

"You're a right bastard." Scottie flipped him off and grabbed his trousers. He stood up, holding the jeans in his hand. "Fine. Where's the cream?"

CHAPTER TWENTY-THREE

SCOTTIE

"Your father needs around-the-clock care, Mr. Monk. He must stop drinking. His health is deteriorating far faster than it should." Dr. Singh clearly thought Scottie didn't understand the seriousness of the situation. She turned toward Silus, who'd just walked out of their dad's hospital room, to bring him into the conversation. "You'll both want to discuss how to proceed with his treatment."

"Could you give us a moment?" Silus asked quietly—and more politely than Scottie could've managed.

Escaping the tense atmosphere by fleeing around the corner, Scottie paced the narrow hallway. His nose twitched at the strong odour of sanitizer. He hated hospitals, doctors, and his old man; it almost made him wish he hadn't insisted on driving by himself without Gray.

"What are we going to do?" Silus joined him, taking a seat in one of the chairs lined up against the wall. "You know he's going to want to go home."

"Let him."

"He'll die, Scottie."

"Let him," Scottie repeated bitterly. He couldn't help thinking it might be better for all of them if they left the old man to it. "The bastard never wants to listen to us anyway."

"But…." Silus frowned in obvious disappointment at him. "He's our father."

"When did the fucker ever do anything paternal for either of us?" Scottie refused to turn the man into a saint because he was dying. "His only act as a parent was donating a bit of sperm and having no idea how condoms work."

"We should be better men than he is." Silus continued to glare stubbornly at him.

"Why?" Scottie had already gone far out of his way to help their father. He'd done his part. "He's going to do whatever the hell he wants. How do you expect to talk him into doing what the doctor wants?"

Silus slumped further into the seat with a sigh. "Do you want to be him? Or do you want to be a better man? Seems to me that you don't have to be just another Monk arsehole."

Twerp has a point, even if he kicked me in the bollocks to make it.

Scottie dropped into the seat next to his brother. "*Fuck.* So, we find a long-term care facility that will take him. It's still only one half of the problem. What's to stop him from checking himself out as soon as our backs are turned?"

"He'll be too sick to escape," his brother pointed out with a wry, but slightly sad smile. "He's dying, Scottie. It isn't about him anymore—it's about me. I don't want to stand at his grave with regrets eating me alive. It's not about him. It's about us."

Scottie swallowed down all the bitter words that his brother didn't need to hear. They'd had this conversation a few times already, and he didn't completely understand where Silus was coming from. He didn't think he'd have even a bit of guilt over walking away from their father, but maybe being a big brother meant sacrificing his anger. "You go see the old arse. I'll see if the doctor has any suggestions."

Less chance of tempers flaring.

After an hour and a half, Scottie managed to coordinate moving his father from his temporary room at the hospital into a more suited facility. By the end of the week, they'd get him settled into the best one available. *Expensive as shit as well. Thank fuck Remi showed me how to handle my money when I retired.* Silus had offered to take on some of the expense, but the kid was in no place to do so.

"I've some money saved," his brother insisted.

"Buy a better car with it." Scottie threw an arm around his brother's shoulders to lead him from the hospital. "Keep your money. How much can you actually have? I've seen your flat."

"Arsehole," Silus grumbled. He grinned sheepishly at Scottie after a few seconds. "Can you give me a lift home? My car broke down on the way here—barely made it to the hospital."

Scottie laughed so hard that he had to bend over with his

hands on his knees to catch his breath. He blocked Silus when he tried to punch him in the arm. "Hand over your keys. I'll get it towed to my friend who runs a repair shop. They'll fix it up for you without duct tape."

"I can manage."

He led his brother out to the car park toward his Jaguar, suddenly glad he'd chosen to drive it and not his repaired motorcycle. "Yeah, but I know how it is to barely manage to pay your bills. I'll fix up the duct tape-mobile."

"Still an arsehole." Silus elbowed him in the side. He tossed his keys over to Scottie. "I'll let you pay for the repairs, but only if you're nicer to Zeb."

Fuck.

"Wait? The fuck? I'm paying to fix your shitty car, and I have to be nice to your shitty date?" Scottie thought he was definitely getting the wrong end of the stick with this agreement. "Why couldn't you have picked someone else to go out with?"

"His cock—"

"Stop." Scottie decided he didn't need to know anything about his little brother's relationship. "I'll try to be nicer if you never mention Zippie's body parts to me again."

"Since when are you a prude? Aren't you the one who sent me graphic comics when Mum's sex talk confused me?" Silus climbed into the passenger seat. "Swanky ride. You know, I'm proud of you for not leaving Dad to rot. I know I didn't suffer the brunt of his drunken rages as a kid. Mum kept me away from him. You've every right to hate him."

"Why don't we grab an early breakfast before I drop you off? We wouldn't want to skip breakfast since we're growing boys." Scottie glared when his brother poked his stomach.

He didn't want to talk about why Silus being proud of him had clogged his throat up for a minute. "Do you have classes today?"

"Nope." Silus played around with the radio. "Zeb said he'd give me a lift tomorrow if my car is still broken down."

"Wonderful."

French fucker.

"He could join us for lunch," Silus teased.

Scottie started the vehicle before smirking over at his brother. "Has your mum met Zippie yet? I bet she'd make the trip up to Cardiff to meet him."

"*Scottie.*"

"I'd even pay for her trip." Scottie had no doubts she'd be unimpressed with her baby boy dating a former rugby player who had a reputation for sleeping around. *Wait, I started that rumour. Shit.* "I'm sure she'd love to see you. And Zippie."

"You're an arse." Silus flipped him off and reached into his pocket to retrieve his mobile. "I'm texting Zeb to say you invited him to lunch."

Ahh fuck.

CHAPTER TWENTY-FOUR

GRAY

October brought slightly cooler weather and more drama of the family variety. Gray had helped Scottie get his father settled into his new home. It hadn't gone smoothly or quietly, but they'd managed it.

It had been impressive to watch the restraint with which Scottie dealt with his father. Gray had a distinct feeling Silus brought out the best in his older brother. They'd all breathed a sigh of relief when the oldest Monk stayed with the doctors.

Let's hope it lasts.

In the weeks since their night at the Red Card, Gray had taken Scottie back twice. Once just for drinks, but the second time they'd indulged in another round of play. They'd also had dinner with Dimas and Leo, the first double date that either of them could ever recall going on.

"You do more than fuck, right?"

The teasing comment from Leo had stuck with Gray. He knew from past experience that building a strong connection with a submissive outside of the bedroom was important. His only response at the time had been to tell the younger Dominant to mind his own business.

A few days later, Gray had reason to question his own sanity. From the looks being sent his way, Scottie felt the exact same way. Who knew all it took to strike fear in the hearts of the two men was a bit of coloured paper and a brightly smiling teacher?

"What are we doing?" Scottie stared at the clump of paper in his hand. "Did we take a knock to the head at some point?"

Gray had a distinct feeling they'd been conned by a certain blue-eyed young woman. "I'm not entirely convinced that we're not hallucinating at this point."

They'd been sharing breakfast with the twins when somehow Alice managed to convince the two of them to attend an origami class. She'd been chased out of it by a couple of the other students making fun of her. Gray couldn't quite believe they'd been talked into it.

Scottie sat practically folded on top of himself in the chair meant more for a ten-year-old than an oversized rugby player. He held up his attempt at origami. "Is this a frog?"

"Sure." Gray glanced down at his own folded paper. "This swan looks like it had a run-in with a lawnmower."

Scottie snorted with laughter before turning away when Alice shushed them. "Fuck."

"Don't swear in front of Alice's friends." Gray started to

stand up, but the chair went with him. "Son of a b… bouillon cube."

"Son of a what?" Scottie coughed his way through what Gray was certain had been another laugh. "Having a bit of a problem with the chair? It appears to be glued to your arse."

Drawing on his years of military service, Gray refrained from yanking the chair off and swinging it at the snickering Scottie. He even managed a "thanks" when he reached over to pry it off him. The small seats had definitely not been meant for men over six foot three.

How the fuck did I get talked into this?

"Something wrong?" Alice looked up from an intricate origami bunny. She'd made enough to start her own farm. "What happened to your swan?"

Gray held up the tortured paper square in his hand. "It's surrealist origami."

"More like de-fucking-constructed origami," Scottie muttered.

Tapping Scottie on the shoulder, Gray nodded his head toward the door. He thought they both required a brief break. They clumsily squeezed between the various tables to make it into the hallway.

"Why are we even here?" Scottie asked once they'd closed the classroom door securely behind them. "Are we doing couple shit now? Are we a couple?"

"Yes."

"Just like that then?"

"You want flowers and a fucking card?" Gray flicked his finger against Scottie's jaw when it dropped. "Want to advertise it in the paper?"

"Are you coming back in?" Alice stuck her head out of the room. "I made another bunny."

"Fuckers do like to multiply," Scottie murmured behind Gray. "Hey kid, how about we buy you stacks of paper and forgo the torture?"

Alice leaned around Gray to stare at Scottie's chest. "My class is here."

"Right. How about a store?" Scottie sounded desperate not to return to the class. "A mountain of paper."

"We'll be right there." Gray ushered Alice back into the room, closing the door again and turning to face his submissive with fire in his eyes. "I do love hearing you beg."

"If you make me hard when I've got to sit through another sodding hour of Mary Poppins in there, I'll kick your arse all the way to London and back." Scottie's scowl evaporated when Gray stalked into his space. "Don't you dare."

Gray smirked wickedly at his submissive, lifting his leg slightly to press between Scottie's thighs. "Careful who you challenge, kitten."

For another excruciatingly long thirty minutes, they sat squashed in the chairs at low tables pretending to make paper animals. Their creations appeared more like road kill than delicate swans. Alice tried to help but mostly giggled at the two of them.

"This is enough to turn me to drink." Scottie lifted his ten attempts at making a frog. "If I squash them together, it might make a tadpole."

Alice darted forward to hug both of them. "Thanks. Bye."

Gray watched her make a quick exit out of the room when the class ended, clearly having met the limit of her ability to socialise in a group setting. "We've been granted a reprieve."

Following Alice, the two men walked slowly out of the building toward the car park across the street. The origami course had apparently been a suggestion from one of her other professors at the university for how she might learn social skills better. Gray didn't think it had been a great success.

"Can you not volunteer us for this shit again?" Scottie threw his leg over his motorcycle and sat down. "Want to go for a drive Saturday?"

"A drive?" Gray picked up his helmet. "On our bikes?"

"It'll be nice enough. We could ride up the A470 through the Brecon Beacons, grab lunch at a pub, and come back to Cardiff with enough time for you to head to Ruck." Scottie stared down at his own helmet, seeming uncharacteristically uneasy. "Just a thought."

"Why don't you sleep over at my place, kitten? We can get up early, fuck in the shower, and have breakfast before we go." Gray thought a ride through a national park sounded perfect after a tiring week at the restaurant. "Follow me home."

"Why?"

Gray stared intently at Scottie for several seconds before replying. "I'm having steak for dinner—and you're going to be the plate."

Despite the bizarre origami course, Gray had greatly enjoyed his day off from Ruck. They'd closed to make changes in the kitchen. He'd left Yara, who'd been promoted to assistant manager, and his sous-chef in charge to ensure the fix went smoothly.

The ride to his cottage gave Gray plenty of time to consider his plans for the evening. He'd purchased a sturdy dining table for a reason. Tonight seemed a good time to give it a full test run.

As they'd had a heavy lunch, Gray decided to cook up a meal that could be eaten by hand. *Licked up easily as well.* His cock hardened almost instantly with visions of a naked Scottie. *Suddenly I'm glad I installed all those hooks on the underside of the table.*

After arriving home, Gray sent Scottie off to shower while he prepared supper. Steak tips in gravy seemed a perfect choice—he had several ideas for what to do with the asparagus he'd bought at the shop. A leftover chocolate pot de crème brought from Ruck the previous night would make for a nice dessert.

Particularly when I lick it off Scottie's dick.

"I'm starved." Scottie joined him in the kitchen in his boxers with a towel in his hand. "What's for supper?"

"You."

"The fuck?"

Taking the towel out of Scottie's hand, Gray looped it around his neck to drag him forward. Their lips connected in a hungry kiss. He controlled the pace; his tongue dipping in to explore his submissive's mouth.

Their teeth clinked together with the force of the kiss. Gray eased back after a moment, catching his breath before biting down on Scottie's bottom lip. *Time to eat.*

"On the table." Gray yanked the towel from Scottie's neck,

twisting it and swatting him on the arse with it. "Up you get."

"You've lost your mind." Scottie stared at the table then back at Gray in surprise when he reached over to drag down his boxers. "You want me to climb on the table starkers? Thought we were having supper."

"I am." Gray spanked Scottie on the arse for the second time. "I won't repeat myself, kitten. Either call a halt or follow orders."

Five minutes later, Gray had Scottie stretched out on his back on the table, secured with kitchen towels including one as a blindfold; a small pillow cushioned his head from the hardwood. He'd been tempted to shove an apple in his mouth to complete the visual.

After ensuring the food had cooled enough, Gray ladled it onto Scottie's chest and stomach. His submissive twitched at the sudden warmth. He bent over him, licking a path through the sauce and picking up a piece of steak.

Dinner is served.

Eating casually off his submissive proved to be a tease for the both of them. Scottie reacted to each new sensation. His hips lifted off the table, trying to hump the air while Gray used an asparagus stalk to play with his nipples and cock.

With his main course finished, Gray grabbed the chocolate from the fridge. He made as much noise as possible in the process, allowing the sounds to surround Scottie. It was another way to heighten the experience for his sight-deprived submissive.

Using his fingers to scoop up some of the pot de crème, Gray smeared it all over Scottie's erection. *The best of both worlds for dessert.* He swirled his tongue around the head of his submissive's shaft. He reached down with his hand to stroke his own cock while continuing to work his mouth.

Gray drew the moment out as long as possible. Scottie writhed under him as the restraints kept him from moving too much. "Are you ready, boy?"

Greatly enjoying the sound of Scottie begging for release, Gray eventually stood up and reached down to use his hand to bring both of them off. It only added to the mess he'd made of his submissive's body.

Gray carefully released Scottie and eased him off the table. "You're dripping on my carpet."

"Why did I have to shower first?" Scottie ran a finger through the food painted on his stomach. "I'm starving. Did you save any for me? Greedy bastard."

Gray grabbed an asparagus stalk that was stuck behind his ear. "You're welcome."

Scottie spun around when a loud sound echoed in the room. They stared at the dining room table as massive crack worked its way across the top. "I'm not paying to fix that."

Chapter Twenty-Five

Scottie

By mid-October, Scottie found himself in the middle of several problems. Gray had gone off with Wyatt, Hamish, and the rest of the retired military crew to the States. A hurricane had hit the Florida coast, leaving one of their friends cut off and in desperate need of help.

It coincided perfectly with Ruck being closed for a week after one of the sous chefs had set the kitchen on fire. They'd barely managed to get it out before the damage claimed the entire restaurant. It would be back up and running in a few weeks, enough time for Gray to fly off to America.

Not that I miss him.

Scottie would've done the same thing for a friend.

Probably.

The biggest issue in his life remained his father, who had somehow managed to get a bottle of scotch into his room. He'd gotten drunk on it, making a mess of the place and a nuisance of himself. Even on his deathbed, his old man could cause trouble for him.

Silus had, of course, inserted himself into the situation. Scottie worked hard to keep his younger brother out of the dramatics. He became grateful to Zeb for providing a suitable distraction.

Who knew Zippie could be so useful?

When his father wouldn't settle down, Scottie had to find yet another medical facility that would take him. He was about ready to wash his hands of it. *How much more time, money, and emotion do I have to waste on the bastard?*

Fucking none.

That's how much.

After strong-arming his father into a new home with new doctors, Scottie quite firmly told him it was his last chance. Silus didn't understand, but his younger brother at least respected that Scottie had reached his limit.

More than anyone else in their family, Scottie had borne the brunt of his father's abusive drunken rages. He'd gone above and beyond already. His therapist had worked with him to manage his anger and need to run for a bottle, but the stress wasn't good for him.

The family angst in many ways kept him from missing Gray. At the same time, it made him miss his Dominant even more. Scottie had grown to depend on him.

Alice: Beard Guy came home. He's sad.
Scottie: Sad? And?
Alice: Make him better.
What am I supposed to do with that text?
Make him better?
With what?
Sex?
Fuck.

Driving through cold and dreary evening weather, Scottie arrived at Gray's place to find Wyatt on his way out the door. The Navy SEAL seemed unusually downcast and went by him with barely a nod. It ratcheted up his concern tenfold.

What the hell happened over there?

Scottie made his way inside the cottage to find Gray sitting in front of the fireplace with his head in his hand. He sat on the sofa beside him. "The twins sent me a text because of their worry over 'beard man.' Do you want to talk about it?"

"An entire community in the Florida Keys was ravaged by a hurricane. No power. Limited resources. Total devastation." Gray leaned back into the cushion with a tired sigh that Scottie could feel in his bones. "I'm going for a run."

"It's pissing down rain outside." Scottie watched, slightly bewildered, while Gray changed quickly into his workout gear and tennis shoes, heading out the door without further comment. "*Idiot.*"

Offering comfort didn't come naturally to him, Scottie sat by the fire for ten minutes before deciding to get off his arse. He wandered around in the kitchen, hunting for something to cook. *One kitchen going up in flames is quite enough. What can I actually manage to fix without burning the house down?*

Of his dubious cooking talents, Scottie managed a full English breakfast brilliantly. Despite the lateness, Gray might appreciate a warm meal. He kept the fireplace stoked as well.

Fuck.

I've gone all domestic.

"What's all this?" Gray trudged into the kitchen with rain dripping off him. His eyes drifted from Scottie to the bacon in the pan. "Let me get dried off, kitten. We can eat by the fireplace."

By the time the food had been plated up, Gray returned wearing a faded USMC T-shirt and sweatpants. He stepped closer to Scottie, pulling him into his arms. He pressed his face against Scottie's neck and breathed in deeply.

"Eggs'll get all weird if we don't eat them now." Scottie didn't know if he should ask what happened again or let Gray tell him in his own time. "Coffee or tea?"

Gray chuckled, causing his beard to rub against Scottie's neck. "Tea. The run cleared my head but chilled me to the bone."

They ate in comfortable silence. The fire crackled and warmed the room. Scottie sank further into the cushions with his plate balanced on his knee.

"My friend and her community lost everything. We pulled people and bodies out of the wreckage." Gray set his plate on the coffee table. "I hate being helpless. My entire life has been dedicated to saving others. We barely scratched the surface in The Keys before they forced us to evacuate."

Over their months together, Scottie had seen the nightmares Gray suffered. The dreams always centred on him failing to save people who in reality he'd rescued. Sometimes when he woke up, he'd talk to Scottie about them.

It had given Scottie a greater appreciation for what Gray, Hamish, Wyatt, and others went through. He'd never really stopped to consider the weight placed on their shoulders. His therapist told him his ability to gain perspective showed how much he'd grown in the past year.

"You tried." Scottie shifted uncomfortably on the couch. "More than I'd do."

Gray nudged him with his elbow. "What if it was Silus?"

"I'd move mountains for him." Scottie didn't think he'd ever be philanthropic, but for his brother, he'd do anything. "Might help you as well."

"*Kitten.*" Gray tilted his head to rest it against the cushion. "I missed you."

They stayed in front of the fire, only moving to stoke it as necessary. Scottie had never found silence to be comforting. With Gray, he managed to relax into the quiet.

Domesticity might not be that bad after all.

CHAPTER TWENTY- SIX

GRAY

After days of cold rain, the sun decided to make a brief appearance. Gray invited Scottie out for a ride. He knew it might be their last for the year as the weather moved deeper into autumn.

Their journey took them along the Welsh coast through small villages and parks. They eventually wound up in a small restaurant Aled had recommended to them. Gray and Scottie had spent quite a bit of time with Wyatt and his husband, as they lived in the same area.

Slowly, Scottie appeared to be learning how to maintain friendships outside of rugby. Gray wondered if he realised how much therapy and staying sober had changed him. His childhood had stunted him in so many ways, and now Scottie was finally beginning to grow up.

"You ever fuck on a bike?" Scottie posed the question casually. "While driving?"

Gray leant forward with his arms resting on the handlebars, turning away from where he'd been checking out the view. They'd pulled off the road onto an overlook not long after leaving the restaurant. "Not while riding. I've never had a death wish."

"And while parked?" Scottie pressed him further.

Gray assessed his submissive in silence for a few seconds, drawing the moment out to frustrate Scottie. "Why don't you use your words, kitten?"

Scottie turned away sharply, becoming overly interested in his gauges. "I've got words."

They danced to this tune each time Scottie wanted to stretch out of his sexual comfort zone. Gray had quickly learned the non-verbal signs. His submissive currently screamed "take me" without saying a thing.

But I want to hear the words anyway.

"Come here, boy." Gray watched while Scottie got off his bike and strode over to stand next to him. "Closer."

When Scottie stood close enough for his legs to brush against him, Gray shot his hand out to catch him by his belt. He slowly unbuckled it before moving on to unbutton his jeans. They might be too exposed for full nudity or intercourse, but being sexually creative was something he excelled at.

His fingers deftly manipulated Scottie's shaft as it began to harden under his touch. Gray stroked him through his briefs at first. He eventually dipped inside them once his submissive thrust up into his hand.

"Good kitten." Gray squeezed the cock in his hand before continuing to stroke. "We could be spotted. Anyone might drive up the road for the view, only to get more than they bargained for. Is that what you wanted? The thrill of being exposed? All your desires bared to the world?"

Scottie's movements stilled several minutes later when a vehicle went past them. Gray continued to feather over his erection. "They'll see us. *Sir.* Fuck."

"They might."

Smirking unworriedly, Gray tugged even harder. The car continued on its way without stopping. Scottie finally grasped Gray's arm for support while his entire body shook.

The road thankfully remained clear while Scottie worked himself to a messy climax. Gray carefully extracted his hand, wiping his fingers on Scottie's briefs before buttoning up his jeans. He didn't envy the long, damp ride home for his submissive.

They kick-started their bikes to head toward Cardiff. Gray enjoyed the rest of the trip. From all the shifting in his seat, Scottie didn't feel the same about it.

"In a hurry, kitten?" Gray chuckled when Scottie rushed by him once he'd opened the door to his cottage. "Drop your clothes in the laundry basket. I'll toss them into the washer while you get cleaned up."

Changing out of his riding gear into a T-shirt and jeans, Gray started the laundry and went barefoot into the living room to get a fire going. He found the cottage grew cold rather quickly in the evenings. With that handled, he wandered into the kitchen to figure out supper.

He'd just gotten ready to start cooking when Scottie walked into the kitchen completely undressed. Gray wondered if they'd reached the stage where they should be keeping a spare set of clothing at each other's place. Or maybe even exchange keys.

With Scottie, serious discussions tended to go one of two ways. He'd either handle it like an adult. *Or, it'll be a complete clusterfuck.* Gray needed a full meal and a cup of coffee before attempting to broach the subject.

Gray opted to leave the conversation for another day. He focused his attention on his naked submissive. "Let's give your mouth a workout before dinner."

Scottie dropped to his knees in front of Gray, reaching up toward the zipper of his jeans. "Yes, sir."

CHAPTER TWENTY-SEVEN

SCOTTIE

November brought bitterly cold rain and even a bit of sleet. It also heralded another blistering article about Gray. His connection to five famous international rugby stars made him and his past newsworthy to tabloids.

They seemed to sense the story surrounding them. A week into November, Scottie had already reached the limit of his patience. He knew how persistent reporters could get.

"Mr. Monk. Mr. Monk?"

Scottie breathed in deeply before locking his Jaguar and turning around to find one of the tabloid journalists rushing up to him. "What?"

"Sources claim you've been spotted at several of the local gay clubs. Any comments?" The reporter stepped into his personal space, holding up the phone to record his response.

"Or, what about your restaurant hiring a chef with a history of perversion?"

No amount of deep breathing cooled the sudden fiery rage in Scottie. He wanted nothing more than to land his fist on the nose of the reporter. His fingernails dug into his palms as he tried to maintain control.

"Do you frequently hire perverts?"

"He's not a pervert," Scottie snapped furiously. "Being gay or being into safe, consensual BDSM isn't a perversion. You closed-minded fuckwitted arsehole."

"Is that Ruck's official statement?" The journalist wisely took a step back from Scottie. "Are all the owners in agreement with your stance on the subject? Is it wise to encourage the perverse?"

Official statement?

"You want an official statement?" Scottie lost all control over his temper. "Here's a scoop for you. I'm gay, and I'm in a committed relationship with the chef at Ruck. Now get the fuck out of my face. If I see one more printed article with ridiculous claims, we'll be suing for defamation."

Stalking down the path toward the club, Scottie wanted to get inside before his temper completely exploded. He didn't mind the nonsense about himself so much. Their attempts to ride Gray into the mud didn't sit well with him.

"Are you into bondage?"

Scottie paused at the entrance to the Sin Bin. He'd been so focused on getting inside that he hadn't realised the reporter was following him. "My preferences are none of your fucking business."

Shutting the door in the man's face, Scottie trudged all the way to his office. He ignored the staff trying to catch his attention. Collapsing into his desk chair, he dropped his head into his hands with a belaboured sigh.

Well, fuck.

In his years of playing rugby, Scottie had struggled with his sexuality. His privacy had also mattered to him. Unlike some of his other friends, he'd taken a little longer to find himself.

Well, I know what's going to be online tomorrow, better text the others to be aware.

Scottie: Had a bit of a row with a journalist. If anyone didn't know I was gay, they certainly do now. We'll be all over the tabloids.

BC: Welcome to the proudly out of the closet club.

Remi: Want us to head to Cardiff to offer support?

Taine: Are you okay? Freddie and I can help run interference at the club if necessary.

Caddock: Calling my solicitor. Tired of these bastards talking shit about all of us. We'll get them to back off.

Gray: I'll bring lunch by once the rush at Ruck is over.

Shutting his mobile off, Scottie decided to avoid the papers completely for a few days. He didn't really understand why their sex life was news in the first place. Unless someone was in the bed with him, what did it matter?

Why is it newsworthy at all?

Who honestly gives a fuck who I'm with?

Jealous bastards. That's who.

"Want to talk about it?" Gray brought Scottie a late lunch

to share at three in the afternoon. "Your bouncer said you've been hiding in your office all day."

"Think I outed myself." Scottie helped to take the wrappings off the plates to reveal sandwiches.

"Were you in the closet?" Gray sounded slightly perplexed. "Neither of us have gone out of our way to hide our relationship."

Scottie shrugged after considering it. "I suppose it's irrelevant now."

Gray sat on the edge of the desk. "What are you upset about?"

Scottie considered the question while taking a bit of his sandwich. "I'm frustrated that they keep hounding you with articles over shit that happened in another country years ago. I don't give a fuck who knows I'm gay. Not really any of their business, is it?"

Gray dragged a chair over to eat lunch at the desk as well. "What's got you fidgeting like I've warmed your ass with my hand, kitten?"

"I outed *us*." Scottie crammed the rest of his sandwich into his mouth to avoid having to say anything else.

"Us?" Gray paused with a chip in his hand. He slowly set it back down on his plate, easing back into the chair to refocus his full attention on Scottie, who couldn't meet his gaze. "You told the reporter about our relationship."

It was a statement—not a question. Scottie found himself nodding yes anyway. He hadn't thought about what Gray's reaction might be to his unguarded moment with the journalist.

"Not sure giving in to them will stop the reporters from

bugging us." Gray brushed crumbs from his shirt. "What exactly did you say to them?"

Scottie shoved a handful of chips into his mouth to avoid answering. He'd strongly defended Gray to the journalist. It embarrassed him a little how ferociously he'd wanted to tell the world about their relationship; something he'd never done before.

"Kitten?"

"Hmm?" Scottie mumbled while trying to choke down his food.

"What did you say?" Gray added a bit more intensity to the question this time.

"You can read it online tomorrow." Scottie had no doubts it would be all over the place.

"Kitten."

"You'll have to wait. Make you want to punish me?" Scottie prodded his Dominant a little. He'd slowly grown more comfortable with the dynamics of their sexual play. "Go on then."

With lunch abandoned on the desk, Gray spent an hour punishing Scottie. They eventually collapsed side by side on the carpet, sweaty and out of breath. Scottie's trousers and briefs dangled from the edge of his desk, out of reach, when the door swung open.

"Oh for God's sake." Taine stood in the doorway, using his body to shield Freddie who tried to peer around him. "Put your damn trousers on so we can talk."

Scottie dropped his head back to the floor with a groan. "Should've locked the door."

"Yes, you bloody should've. At least cover yourself." Taine raised a hand to cover his eyes. "Caddock's got his solicitor to recommend someone in Cardiff who will be here shortly to discuss not only a cease and desist letter but also the odds of winning if we file against the papers for defamation and libel. Now put your trousers on before I lose my lunch."

"You barged into my office." Scottie got to his feet and smirked at Taine, who backed out of the room, shutting the door behind him. "His face was a fucking picture."

"Get dressed, kitten." Gray tossed him his boxers and trousers before pulling his own clothes back on. "And Scottie?"

"Yes?"

"I'm proud to claim you as my own."

CHAPTER TWENTY-EIGHT

GRAY

RETIRED RUGBY PLAYER IN RELATIONSHIP WITH RETIRED AMERICAN MARINE.

As headlines went, Gray didn't mind the one greeting him when he opened the link Hamish and Wyatt had both gleefully emailed to him. *Fucksticks.* Caddock's solicitor appeared to have made at least a small impression on the papers. The article was far kinder and less sensationalised than all the ones before it had been.

Of all the rugby players, Caddock had the least tolerance for the press. He'd apparently worked hard to shut them down when they'd begun to follow his young nephew around at school. It was easy to understand why the man refused to play games with journalists.

He was on his second cup of coffee when a timid knock had him going to answer the door. "Alice. Alex. Up early this morning, I see."

The twins shuffled a bit before stepping into the cottage. They made their way into the kitchen, sitting on the stools around the island. He smiled at the two whispering together while he started to make breakfast.

"Beard guy?"

Gray glanced over his shoulder to find Alex had bravely stepped over to him. "Triangle toast this morning?"

"Yes." Alex nodded repeatedly. Both twins preferred their bread cut into triangles; they liked square edges on things. "Are you okay?"

Gray blinked at the question that he'd barely heard, what with Alex whispering it with his head down. "I'm fine."

"Sure?" Alice darted over to stand beside her brother, identical looks of concern in their pale blue eyes. "It's okay to be not all right."

Gray turned away from the stove to stare at the twins. "Did you two read the article about Scottie and me this morning?"

"Maybe," Alice said while her brother nodded yes again.

Before he could address the twins' concerns, another knock on the door interrupted. Scottie wandered by to answer it—dressed in his jeans and one of Gray's USMC T-shirts. He returned to the kitchen a few seconds later with his brother, Silus.

"It's the wonder twins." Silus waved at the two blonds before grinning cheerfully at Gray, who gave a sigh of resignation before pointing him toward one of the empty stools. His smile widened with the offer of breakfast. "I'm a university student. I never say no to free food."

Gray put Alex in charge of the toast while Scottie poured coffees for everyone—except Alice, who wanted tea. He wondered in amusement when he'd adopted three grown-up children. "We're having bacon, sausage, and a mushroom and Fontina frittata. Any complaints?"

Four heads shook in unison to give him his answer. It was clear from the hushed conversation between the brothers that Silus had seen the article as well. He'd apparently gone to Scottie's flat first, then to Gray's cottage when he couldn't reach either of them on their phones.

"I told you to turn your phone on." Gray chose to ignore the fact that he'd left his off as well. "We'll be overrun with people by the time I'm done with breakfast. You better put more coffee on the pot and hand me some more bacon."

In the short time it took him to get the frittata in the oven, Gray's prediction proved to be accurate. Even though they'd immediately turned their phones back on, many of their friends dropped in to check on them. Only the ones who'd known about the article beforehand stayed away.

The majority of them left relatively quickly to get to work, though they all managed to steal food on their way out. Aled and Wyatt chose to stay to eat breakfast with them. Gray grumbled but had to admit the show of solidarity touched him. Alice and Alex disappeared into the garden with their plates, overwhelmed by all the unexpected interruptions; the autistic twins didn't handle changes to their normal routine well.

How the hell has breakfast with me become part of their routine?

"Tell the A-team to meet me in my greenhouse whenever they're ready." Aled thanked Gray for breakfast and dragged his husband out of the cottage. "No rush, though. I'm sure they'll need some time to calm their nerves."

"I'm going to be late for class." Silus stole the last piece of toast and frittata from Scottie's plate. He dodged his brother, who made a grab for his breakfast, and raced for the door. "Thanks for the food."

"We'll do the dishes." Alice reappeared with her brother close behind. She picked uneasily at the dishrag in her hand for a minute. "Are we in the way? We can leave."

Gray's brow furrowed at the obviously uneasy twenty-year-olds. "You're both welcome in my cottage any fucking time of the day or night."

"Maybe not when we're actually fucking, though." Scottie leaned forward to whisper in his ear so only Gray could hear him.

Gray placed his hand over Scottie's face and shoved him out of the kitchen while the twins giggled behind him. "Go get changed."

"Beard guy?"

After Scottie disappeared down the hall, Gray spent several minutes alleviating the concerns of the two autistics. He wanted them to feel welcome in his home. They eventually settled down, but still insisted on doing the dishes for him.

Running late himself, Gray joined Scottie in the shower. He barely had enough time to actually wash and change. The twins had cleaned up and left when they returned to the kitchen.

When Gray arrived at Ruck, he gratefully accepted the coffee his manager handed to him. He'd apparently brought drinks for everyone. They had their daily meeting about the upcoming menu plans. He believed clear communication kept the restaurant running smoothly.

With the meeting out of the way, Gray started to prepare the tasting for the staff. He ensured everyone had a bit of what they'd be serving throughout the week. It helped them explain the menu to customers better.

"Voodoo?" Gray spotted the former Navy SEAL, Cole Willis, who worked with Wyatt and Hamish, chatting up Yara by the front door. "She is *way* too good for you."

Cole flipped him off cheerfully before winking at Yara. "See you at six."

Gray watched the six-foot-three Haitian-American saunter out of the restaurant. He glanced over to find Yara watching Cole leave. "Military men are nothing but trouble."

"Aren't you one of them?" Yara smiled brightly at him. "He's lovely."

Gray pinched the bridge of his nose. *Young love.* "Careful with his heart. I'd hate to see a grown man sobbing on my doorstep."

"His heart?"

Gray pointed toward the now closed front door. "He'll lose both his head and his heart over you."

"I'll be kind," Yara promised with a laugh.

Leaving young love to run its course without his interference, Gray made his way back to the kitchen to start his prep for the day. He couldn't quite shake the feeling that they hadn't heard the last of the drama from the morning news. Nothing he could do about it in any case.

"Gray? Are you in here?"

"In the walk-in." Gray continued grabbing ingredients and placing them into the large pan that he'd grabbed on the way into the freezer. He stepped out to find Hamish waiting for him. "Go away, Hamster. I'm busy."

"Nice. Here I am doing a favour for you, and you tell me to bugger off." Hamish held up a bag, which he shook gently. "Akash sent over a bunch of spices for you. Shall I take them back?"

"I'm attempting a few new dishes this coming week. Your better half offered to share some of his inventory with me." Gray grabbed the bag before setting it on the stainless steel countertop with the rest of the ingredients. "Well? What's on your mind? You didn't come here to play gofer."

"I might've."

Leaving Hamish to his thoughts, Gray started prepping the ingredients. It took almost a full five minutes before the silence was broken. His old boss cleared his throat a few times before Gray finally set his knife down.

"What?"

"Are you serious about Monk?" Hamish held his hands up when Gray swung around to glare at him. "Easy. I'm not making judgements about him. Did you read what he said to the reporter?"

With a tired groan, Gray reached the absolute limit of his patience of hearing about the article. It had been a topic of conversation all through breakfast. He had no intention of spending the rest of the day dealing with it.

"You have an office, Ross. This isn't it. Get your ass out of my kitchen." Gray turned his back on Hamish, picking up the knife to continue prepping. "Well? I can still hear your breathing."

"I'm not making any judgements," Hamish insisted.

"Did I say you did?" Gray cleared his throat roughly. "Look, I know you and Scottie didn't exactly get off to a great start. Fuck. He was a complete asshole to Akash. I'm not going to claim he's magically become Mother Theresa, but he's grown up quite a bit. I don't owe you or anyone else an explanation of how serious our relationship is."

"Defensive much, old man?"

Gray set his knife down for a second time and returned his full attention to Hamish. "We're both too old for this shit."

CHAPTER TWENTY-NINE

SCOTTIE

The sun hadn't even risen when Scottie stood at the large window looking out into Gray's garden with a coffee mug in hand. Messages had begun to come into his phone around three in the morning and hadn't stopped. He'd given up on sleep around five, not seeing the point.

Should've just turned the thing off and been done with it.

In the beginning, all of the messages came from his father filled with vile words about his own son being gay. Scottie ignored the lot of them, eventually deleting the thread and blocking his old man's number. Around four in the morning, his brother had texted him—followed shortly by a few of his other relatives.

It seemed that in a fit of temper, his father had managed to send himself into a heart attack, his body already weakened by cirrhosis and decades of poor living. Scottie knew he'd be judged harshly by some of his family for not immediately rushing to the hospital, but after thirty-plus years of abusive behaviour, he just felt numb to everything.

"What's got you up so early?" Gray joined him in the kitchen, pouring coffee for himself and setting Scottie's mobile on the counter. "Your damn phone keeps buzzing. Is everything okay?"

Scottie stretched his arm out to grab the phone. He scrolled through the messages from family members who'd never bothered to contact him before, and eventually found one from Silus. "My old man took a turn for the worse."

Gray moved up beside him, looping an arm around Scottie's back. "How bad is it?"

"He died an hour ago." Scottie twisted his phone so they could both read the text from his younger brother. "Fuck. Fuck. *Fuck.*"

"What do you need?"

"You to fuck me until I can't remember any of this shit." Scottie dropped his phone on the counter and downed the last of his now cold coffee. "This is such bullshit."

Gray shook his head while keeping his arm firmly around him. "You can't sex your way out of this, kitten. Let's get showered and dressed. You might not give a shit about your old man, but Silus needs his big brother."

With a frustrated grunt, Scottie tossed the mug into the sink, barely avoiding breaking it. He shrugged out from under Gray's arm to trudge down the hall into the bedroom. His shower lasted long enough to soap up and rinse off—more perfunctory than anything else.

He found Gray had already showered in the en suite in his spare bedroom. They dressed in silence. His emotions were too chaotic and tense to make conversation a good idea.

The first cold snap of the winter season had hit Cardiff early. They both grabbed jackets and quickly got into the Jaguar. Gray took the keys out of his hand, likely worried Scottie might be too distracted to drive.

"You ready for this?"

Scottie jolted in his seat, taking a few minutes to realise they'd arrived at the hospital. "Fuck."

Gray rested a hand on the back of Scottie's neck to squeeze firmly. "Have you thought about the funeral?"

"Toss him in the sea and be done with it." Scottie yanked the door open and stormed out of the vehicle. He didn't want comfort; he wanted two bottles of scotch. "Do they still do burials at sea?"

"Not sure your dad would qualify." Gray caught up with him as they walked into the hospital. "Did you text your brother?"

"Scottie." Silus rushed over to them, interrupting before Scottie could answer. "Thank heavens. I can't deal with all these Monks."

Scottie smothered his inappropriate urge to laugh at the harried look on his brother's face. "What the hell have I been telling you about them? You should be glad your mum kept you sheltered from the Monk madness."

"They keep asking me if I'm paying for the funeral. How am I supposed to do that?" Silus grabbed Scottie by the shirt to start leading him down the hall past the receptionist's desk. "I have duct tape on my car. I'm a university student—your marine feeds me half the time."

"Retired marine," Gray interjected.

"You're not paying for a thing." Scottie had been primed for an argument for days. He had no problems taking his entire family down a notch if it meant they'd leave his brother alone. "Fuckers."

Silus rushed forward to step in front of him. "No screaming in the hospital."

"Yeah, yeah." Scottie rolled his eyes at his brother. "Don't get shirty with me. I'll pull the duct tape off your piece of shit car."

"Arsehole." Silus shoved Scottie, and the two devolved into a mock battle until Gray cleared his throat. "Right. Hospital. Sadness. No fun."

"Scott."

Scottie almost instinctually stepped between his brother and his uncle. He had few good memories of his father's oldest sibling. "Bernie."

"Show some respect." His uncle Bernard had aged considerably since the last time they'd seen each other. "You were always a little piece of shit kid."

"If you want me to pay for the funeral, you'll show me some respect." Scottie knew without asking that no one in his family could afford to pay for a single flower, let alone everything else. He pushed Silus towards Gray. His uncle seemed to be fighting with himself. "Where's his doctor? Bernie?"

While Gray played guard for Silus, Scottie followed his uncle down the hall. His extended family cluttered the area around what had been his father's room. *Vultures.* He hadn't seen most of them in almost ten years; they'd all learned quickly that he wouldn't play ATM for them.

When Scottie's career took off, they'd all clamoured around him wanting to ride on his coattails. They'd wanted handouts constantly. He'd told them all to get stuffed, not that it completely stopped them from asking.

The only person in their family to receive any money from him was Silus. His younger brother deserved it. None of the other Monks deserved anything other than to be tossed into the rubbish.

And of all of their family, Silus had been the one to never once ask him for anything.

Several exhausting hours later, Scottie had the medical certificate from the doctor. He'd also convinced Silus to leave with him instead of staying with their toxic relatives. Gray drove them across the city to the nearest register office to get the documents filled out to apply for the Certificate for Burial.

A few days later, Scottie hired a funeral director to handle the arrangements. His initial thought to simply cremate his father and dump the ashes down the loo was overruled by Silus. The service would be small—but they'd have one at the church near the cemetery where the man would be buried.

Given his father had no earthly possessions worth anything; there'd been no fighting over a will. The rest of the family managed to behave with some semblance of decency, at least in his presence. Scottie hadn't thought it possible.

All of his friends flew into Cardiff for the funeral. Scottie insisted he'd be fine. They ignored him.

"It's okay to be angry, kitten." Gray leaned against the side of the church. The priest had promised the service would be simple and respectful. "He was a bastard who did everything in his power to hurt you when he should've protected you."

"Fucking arsehole." Scottie knew his temper had gotten perilously close to erupting. He'd even snapped at several of his staff at the club until Taine insisted he take a few days off. "Why am I even here? The bastard wouldn't have spit on me if I were on fire. He donated sperm, and that comprises his sole contribution to being a parent."

To his credit, Gray didn't offer pointless words of comfort. Scottie knew from past conversations that both of their childhoods hadn't been ideal. Of everyone in his life, Gray likely understood more than anyone how conflicted he felt.

Scottie shoved his hands into his pockets—less chance of him taking a swing—and forced himself to enter the church. "Let's get this shit over with."

He made it through ten minutes of the whimpering, mournful tears from aunts and uncles who usually thought a family reunion meant screaming at each another. He found it hard to stomach their hypocrisy.

When the priest began going on about what a "good man Scott George Monk" had been, Scottie made for the door. He'd paid for the funeral and saw no reason to sit through an hour of lies. The door slammed shut behind him with a heavy thud.

So much for not making a scene.

Despite his best efforts, it was impossible to pretend his father had been anything other than a drunken, abusive man. Their entire family ignored what happened inside their home. Scottie couldn't bring himself to be bothered if they thought the worst of him.

They hadn't minded the bruises on his face as a child. Scottie remembered quite clearly wanting help. They'd all turned their backs on him.

The family code of silence.

It's not our place to say anything. You just have to learn not to anger him, dearie. He's a good man who's had a hard life.

Fuck 'em if they want to get on their high horse.

"Why don't we just leave?"

Scottie glanced up to find BC, Taine, Remi, Caddock, and their significant others had followed him out of the church. Gray followed a few seconds later with Silus behind him. "Anyone actually left inside?"

"Arseholes who don't mind the lies." BC shrugged. "The Sin Bin's closed for the day. Why don't we have our own service there?"

"Taine going to play priest?" Caddock suggested, only to be punched in the arm by the man in question. "What? You're the adopted son of one—you're more qualified than any of us heathens. We only darken the doors of a church for weddings, funerals, and Christmas celebrations."

"You're all heathens." Remi drew his wife, Sarah, back into his arms, resting his chin on top of her bright red hair. "The club would provide a friendlier and more comfortable atmosphere for you to mourn however you wish."

"Mourn?" Scottie scoffed, ignoring the glare from his brother. "I'll grieve by taking a shit on his grave."

"*Scottie.*"

"Sorry." Scottie pulled Silus into a hug. He'd tried his hardest to avoid losing his temper in front of his brother. "We'll be more comfortable at the club."

And it has plenty of alcohol.

I could use a drink—or twenty.

Right. Not supposed to drink.

The past week had severely tested Scottie's resolve to stay sober. He'd skipped his appointment with his therapist. None of it seemed to matter amidst all the upheaval after his father's death.

They separated into their vehicles to head for the Sin Bin. Gray and Silus joined Scottie in his Jaguar. He'd promised himself to keep a close eye on his younger brother, who seemed affected by the loss.

And his mum'll kick my arse all across the city if I don't.

Silus leaned forward in the back seat to place a hand on Scottie's shoulder. "I'm sorry."

"What do you have to be sorry about?" He fought to get the key in the ignition before finally getting the Jaguar started. "You hit your head on something?"

"Don't be an arse." Silus slapped him on the shoulder. "I'm sorry that you had to pay for the funeral. I know you did it for me. You'd have cremated him and thrown his ashes in the nearest rubbish bin. This is healthier for both of us. Maybe over time, you'll realise it."

Doubtful.

Scottie shrugged.

"Look at it this way." Silus shifted back into his seat. "The grave gives you somewhere to go to yell at him."

"Kid has a point," Gray added. "Or, you might never visit it."

"Would you?" Scottie asked after a few minutes' silence.

"I don't know." Gray reached forward to adjust the temperature. "It's easy for me to say I would, but some of those foster families—I'd never even go to their funeral, let alone their grave. Do what works for you. No one can tell you how to grieve or how to heal. Same goes for you, kid. You might both mourn in your own ways. It doesn't make either one of you right or wrong."

"He's smart." Silus gave Gray two thumbs up.

I'll mourn with a bottle of the strongest liquor I can find. Or five.

The atmosphere at the club stifled him almost as much as the church. Scottie had gone from being surrounded by the fake grief of his extended family to the sincere concern of his friends. None of them grasped how much he wanted space to simply forget.

His well-meaning friends had all, for the most part, enjoyed their childhoods. Maybe not idyllic, but certainly not as violently abusive as his own had been. Their parents supported them in their endeavours. Even Silus, his own brother, hadn't truly known the depths of their father's issues.

Sitting by himself at the bar, Scottie enjoyed a brief moment of not being asked how he felt. The question seemed to be on every single person's lips. They didn't bother with anything else.

How are you doing?

How are you feeling?

Telling himself they meant well didn't really help. If they wanted to do him a good turn, a bottle of whisky and bit of privacy would be brilliant. He knew the odds of getting either were slim to none.

"Want to shoot something?" Gray took a seat beside him. He set a mug of tea in front of Scottie. "Drink up, kitten. Hamish swears this stuff makes everything better."

Not without an entire bottle of scotch in it.

"Why would I want to shoot something?" Scottie ignored the tea for a moment. He wanted to chuck it at someone's head. "Only person I've ever wanted to hurt is dead and buried."

Gray placed a hand on his shoulder. "The anger fades."

"Does it?"

CHAPTER THIRTY

GRAY

"Gray?"

Gray excused himself from the conversation with Remi and Sarah to find Silus fidgeting nervously with Zeb hovering behind him. They'd all hung out together for the last few hours after the funeral. "What's wrong?"

"Scottie took off in his Jag, and he's not answering my calls." Silus waved his phone around as if to provide proof. "Zeb can give me a ride—but I'm worried about Scottie. He's not as stoic as he claims to be about all of this."

Promising to check on Scottie, Gray left Silus to be comforted by Zeb. He'd actually been impressed by the maturity of both men. They acted more like adults than some of the people around them who were ten years older or more.

As Scottie had been his ride to the funeral, Gray caught

a ride with Wyatt and Aled. They dropped him off in front of Scottie's flat. He'd rightly assumed his submissive would retreat to his place.

"Oi. Aren't you friends with Monk?"

Gray paused on the stairs to find one of Scottie's neighbours blocking his path. "I am. Something wrong?"

"He's blasted music for over an hour now, and it sounds like he's tearing down the walls as well. I thought about calling the police, but maybe you can get him to settle down." She edged by Gray to continue down the steps. "Is everything all right?"

Deciding not to encourage neighbourly nosiness, Gray walked the last bit up to Scottie's place, repeatedly knocking on the door. He banged on it in an attempt to be heard over the volume of the music. From the crashing, it seemed safe to assume furniture was being tossed around the apartment.

A thud that felt like it shook the floor made Gray glance up in concern. He banged on the door again with no response. *Damn it. I should've kept a closer eye on him at the funeral.*

It didn't take a genius to grasp how his father's death had messed with Scottie's emotions. He likely struggled with the loss of a family member who'd been abusive and cruel. Any thought of closure had disappeared into the grave.

Gray could relate. He'd gone to great lengths to work through his own issues with his foster parents. Even now in his fifties, there were still days when anger simmered deep within him; he'd learned with time how to keep the emotions from controlling him.

Closure never really happens. What can an abusive parent say? Sorry?

No apology had ever made anything better for Gray. He imagined it wouldn't for Scottie either. In his experience, sorry usually only made the one asking for forgiveness feel better.

Gray had made a conscious decision to allow his bitterness and anger to go. His foster parents had all but ruined his childhood; they didn't deserve to continue to control his life as an adult. He hoped to somehow encourage Scottie to reach the same conclusion—or get him to talk with his therapist.

Raucous singing to an Aerosmith song interrupted his thoughts and his knocking. *Oh for fuck's sake.* Gray had a sneaking suspicion that Scottie had jumped off the sobriety wagon into a bucket of whisky. It was going to be an incredibly long afternoon trying to sober him up.

"Open the door." Gray banged his fist against it once again, hard enough to shake it on its hinges. "Scottie."

Cursing followed yet another crash before the music finally went down to less deafening levels. Scottie eventually appeared, leaning heavily against the open door. He peered blearily at Gray as he swayed on his feet.

"How much have you had to drink?" Gray eased forward, which forced Scottie to retreat into his flat. He glanced around the living room to find much of it wrecked. "You don't do things by halves, do you? Is there anything you didn't completely destroy?"

"Fucking had it coming." Scottie stumbled over the remnants of his coffee table and landed somewhat safely on the sofa, which was missing several cushions and partially covered in what Gray hoped was alcohol. "Shit. My arse is wet."

Gray muffled his snort of his amusement. "What—"

Scottie shot up off the couch before Gray managed to complete his thought. "Fucking bastard's dead. Used to wish he'd die. Drink himself to death. Guess he did."

"Scottie." Gray approached the volatile drunk as he would a caged lion. "How much have you had to drink?"

"Fuck if I know." Scottie sounded more lost than enraged. "I found a bottle stashed away."

The slightly confused tone evaporated in the next second when Scottie screamed in an almost primal rage. It reminded Gray of the time one of his marines had found a friend wounded on the battlefield. His attention returned to Scottie when he dropped to his knees, slamming his fists into the carpet.

Gray leapt across the broken table to get to him. He wrapped his arms tightly around Scottie. "Easy, kitten. You'll get through this. Don't bottle it all up."

"What do you know about it?" Scottie struggled against him before eventually wilting in his arms. "Why do I even care? He wouldn't have given two shits if I died unless I'd put him in my will."

The ranting continued for a good ten minutes. Scottie finally trailed off when his voice went hoarse. He sounded perilously close to tears.

"Why the fuck does it even matter?" Scottie tried to stand up, but Gray kept a hold of him.

Gray shifted slightly, so the broken leg of the table stopped prodding him up the arse. "You care because the fantasy of having a good father has disappeared. You clung to the hope that all abused children can't seem to completely shake.

I know, because I've been there. The trouble is that now your dad's gone and all you have left are bad memories and unresolved issues."

"Profound shit." Scottie turned his head to the right and proceeded to become violently ill over their legs. "*Shit.*"

Why the hell didn't I have Wyatt drop me off at my cottage?

Right.

Relationships.

Dragging them both out of the muck, Gray strong-armed Scottie down the hall into his bedroom. He stripped them both out of their clothes and moved into the shower. *A nice icy cold one.* It served to sober his submissive up a little.

Over the next hour, Gray managed to clean up the living room. Scottie stayed slumped on a chair, completely naked, staring at the floor. He'd wanted sex, but Gray refused.

And he planned to continue to say no until Scottie had completely sobered up and spoken to his therapist about his father's death. Sex, in Gray's opinion, could be used as a crutch to take the place of alcohol—or any other coping mechanisms—but he thought in his submissive's case it would do more damage. The destruction of the living room proved the need for him to work through his anger.

No intense sex while emotionally compromised.

Angry people tended to make bad decisions.

Not in the bedroom.

Not with me.

I'll take care of my almost lion—sex can wait.

CHAPTER THIRTY-ONE

SCOTTIE

The morning after the funeral, Gray had driven Scottie straight to his therapist. He'd brooked no arguments. The two-hour session helped exorcise some of the rage in his heart, but not all of it.

Three more sessions through the following week helped as well. Scottie didn't feel magically changed, but alcohol had stopped its siren call—so maybe it helped more than he thought.

After clearing out and replacing his busted furniture, Scottie tracked down Silus at his university. He'd gotten so lost in his own thoughts that he'd neglected to check on him. His brother appeared to be completely fine, aside from Zeb being attached to his hip.

"Monk." Zeb tried to catch up to him on the way to the car park. "Will you slow down?"

"Yes, Zippie?" Scottie turned around to lean against his vehicle with his arms folded across his chest. "What can I do for France?"

Zeb muttered curses in French for a few seconds before seeming to rein in his temper. "I am not going to hurt your brother."

"You're both young. Of course you're going to fucking hurt each other." He couldn't help a laugh at Zeb's expense. "Did you chase me down to tell me that?"

"Yes."

"We're never going to be friendly." Scottie quickly continued to avoid Zeb shooting off at the mouth. "Do right by Silus, and I'll forget what a wanker you are."

"How generous," Zeb remarked mockingly. "Should I say thank you?"

"Fucking…." Scottie trailed off, catching sight of his brother approaching over Zeb's shoulder. "I won't be an arsehole if you won't. How about it?"

Zeb held his hand out after several tense seconds. "*Merde.*"

"Playing nicely, are we?" Silus sidled up to Zeb, glowering suspiciously at his brother. "Weren't you heading off to see Gray? Changed your mind?"

"Zippie wanted a word." Scottie tried and failed not to poke at Zeb a little. He really did bring out the worst in him. "Don't you have class?"

"Why don't you have a coffee with us?" Silus placed a hand on Zeb's arm while giving Scottie another glare. "I've an hour before my next class. C'mon, big brother, don't you want to get to know my boyfriend better?"

No, I don't.

Wait.

Did he say boyfriend?

Bugger.

With a resigned groan, Scottie followed the lovebirds across campus to a small café crowded with students. They grabbed coffee and a few pastries before stepping outside to find a quieter spot to sit in the almost bitterly cold breeze. Silus appeared determined to bridge the gap between his brother and his boyfriend.

Not fucking likely.

I could try harder.

Drinking coffee had never gone so slowly. Silus looked ready to rip his hair out. Scottie smothered the guilt in his belly. He wasn't making it easier on his brother and decided to make a run for it.

Silus followed him out to his Jaguar. "He's brilliant, Scottie. He makes me happy. Thinks I'm smart but doesn't take the mickey when I'm rambling about computers."

Scottie scowled at the unintentional reminder of the teasing and bullying Silus had dealt with as a young teenager. "I'm not the one going out with him. Why does it matter if we get along?"

"Remember Dad's funeral? Of course, you do, stupid question." Silus waved a hand to stop Scottie from answering. "Seeing all this family who couldn't be bothered to get to know me. They barely acknowledged me at all. Some even said nasty things about Mum and me. It made me realise aside from my mother and you—I don't have a family. It's not too much to ask for you to be a bit nicer to Zeb."

Scottie got yet another punch of guilt to his stomach at the sadness in his brother's eyes. "All right, all right, turn off the pout. I'll do better with Zippie. I promise. I'll even call him Zeb."

To his face.

He planned to do his best, at least, at being nicer.

Leaving the university, Scottie drove straight to Ruck. He planned to visit briefly with Gray before checking in at the club. They had a fancy dress event scheduled for the upcoming weekend, and everything had to be set up for it.

Once parked in his usual spot, Scottie hopped out only to pause at the sight of Remi and his wife waiting nearby. *Brilliant. It's going to be Frenchie part deux.* Sarah waved at him before heading into the restaurant. He found a stern-faced Frenchman blocking his path.

"Frenchie." Scottie didn't think he'd done anything to tick Remi off recently. He'd been mostly on his best behaviour, aside from the day of the funeral. "What've I buggered up to earn your disapproval?"

"We want to talk." Remi caught him by the shoulder to forcibly guide him away from Ruck toward the Sin Bin entrance instead. "Gray will have lunch delivered for us in an hour or so. Depends on how quickly they start serving at the restaurant."

"Oh for fuck's sake." Scottie tripped over the carpet in the foyer of the club. Remi led him into the first-floor space where all of his old rugby mates were seated around the largest of the tables. "Is this an intervention? Seriously? After I had one bad night?"

"Sit." Remi pushed him into one of the empty seats. "We drove all the way to Cardiff—so sit and listen without cheek."

So it was an intervention. Another one. Scottie counted to ten several times to avoid snapping at the well-meaning idiots. He appreciated how much they obviously cared about him even if he wanted to bash them all upside the head.

He thought it unlikely Gray had reached out to them. His visits to the therapist had eased his Dominant's concerns. It made him wonder who'd talked to his friends and what was said to worry them enough to make the trip to Cardiff.

"Drinking isn't the answer to dealing with the pain of your father's death." Taine started what clearly had to be a prepared conversation. He stopped when Scottie started to snicker. "This isn't funny. Don't be an arse. We're only concerned about you. You've done so well since you left rehab."

"Fuck off. I'm not being an arse—not this time." Scottie couldn't deny he'd gone out of his way to be difficult in the past. "You're working yourselves up without having all the information. I've seen my therapist three or four times since the funeral. And I haven't touched a drop of alcohol outside of one night when I got drunk."

"Really?"

"Oh?"

"Good."

"Well, that's brilliant."

"Is that your joint opinion?" Scottie laughed when they all responded at the same time with smiles of relief. *Idiots.* "Not falling back into that boozy nightmare again. Not if I can help it."

And he wasn't planning to ever again.

The clarity that came with sobriety had, not to sound clichéd, changed his life completely. Scottie saw no reason to throw it all away for a supposed good time. His friends clearly had no intention of allowing him to slip either.

Just a year or two ago, their attempted intervention would've angered him to the point of getting into a fight. Scottie actually found himself grateful for the obvious evidence of their worry for him. His health mattered to his friends enough for them to risk his temper flaring as it so often had in the past.

"You're all morons." Scottie hid a smirk when they all tensed at what he'd say next. "Thanks for caring enough to do this."

Caddock narrowed his eyes on Scottie. "Should we check him for a fever? I can't remember him ever saying thank you before."

Scottie flipped him off with both middle fingers. "Gray claims you make family where you can when life gives you a shit one at the start. I suppose you're all included in mine."

"He called us family." BC nudged Remi with his elbow. "Can we get it in writing? Scottie Monk said something soppy."

"And instantly regretted it." Scottie decided one emotional revelation was enough for the rest of the day—maybe even the year.

Lunch arrived shortly after to break up their continued joking. Over the meal, they nattered on about all their news. BC had the greatest news: Graham had been once again declared cancer-free at his annual follow-up with the doctor. They all cheered for him.

"How about you and your American?" Taine's question had all eyes shifting to Scottie. "Are you two getting serious? Is it *official*?"

"Officially what?" Scottie shrugged, trying to seem completely indifferent. "We're good."

Remi leaned forward in his seat, setting his fork down. "Good?"

"Good. Opposite of bad. The fuck do you want from me? An analysis of my relationship?" Scottie refused to dissect what he had with Gray for his friends. "Eat your lunch. I'm done gossiping with you lot."

"I do believe Scottie's in love," BC teased him.

Deciding to be the mature adult that he was, Scottie spooned up some of the mashed potatoes to flick them straight into BC's face. The food fight was short-lived and brutal. They only stopped when one of his managers rushed out to yell at them while they cackled with laughter like naughty schoolboys caught by their teacher.

Remi pulled Scottie aside once order had been restored. "Gray's good for you."

"You've half a pickle in your hair." Scottie went up the stairs and down the hall toward his office where he kept a spare change of clothes. "Are you following me for a reason?"

Remi didn't respond to his aggressive tone in kind. "Are you two serious?"

"*Remi.*"

"Are you happy with him?" Remi stayed by the door while

Scottie hunted down the bag with his clean T-shirt and jeans. "You've been a miserable bastard for so many years."

Scottie ripped off his dirty shirt and flung it toward Remi. "Yes, Mum. I'm happy. He's happy. Go bother someone else."

Honestly.

Remi deflected the shirt toward the chair in the corner. "We care about you."

"I'm aware." Scottie pulled on his clean shirt before starting to get his shoes off. "What does that have to do with fuck all?"

Remi pinched the bridge of his nose before breathing out noisily. "One day you might learn how to be a friend."

"Right. One day. But can I get dressed first?"

CHAPTER THIRTY-TWO

GRAY

"They had a food fight."

Gray glanced over his shoulder to find Yara with a tray of stacked dishes. "Did they?"

"Made a mess of the dance floor." She grinned at him. "I'm taking my break before the next group arrives."

Gray's eyes narrowed when she checked her reflection in the stainless steel fridge. "Expecting a visitor?"

"Cole." Yara danced out of the kitchen with a wave.

To his surprise, Cole and Yara had continued to date. They went out a few times a week. He even planned to introduce her to his parents when they came for a visit in December.

Hope it goes well.

They both deserve happiness.

With a shake of his head, Gray decided to mind his own business. He'd stayed out of the budding romance once certain

Cole would treat Yara right. The only relationship he wanted to focus on was his own.

Leaving the empty dishes for his kitchen staff to handle, Gray refocused his attention on the brown butter roast chicken that he'd prepared. He'd be turning the meat, once shredded, into miniature pot pies. The colder weather had everyone wanting something warm and comforting.

"Taste *everything*." Gray had to remind one of his newer assistants, who'd been sent over from the culinary course to intern. "Flavour is all about layers of seasoning."

At times, Gray felt more like a culinary teacher than an executive chef. He enjoyed it immensely—though not enough to admit to either Hamish or Wyatt that their invitation to Cardiff had changed his life for the better. Their egos didn't need any encouragement.

"Mr. Beard. Mr. Beard."

"It's *Baird*," Gray repeated for the hundredth time for his newest employee, one of the three valets, who couldn't seem to get his name straight. "*Baird* like bear with a d or bared."

"Right. Beard."

Gray decided to pick his battles. "Shouldn't you be outside?"

"Yara's boyfriend told me to come find you." He gestured for Gray to follow him.

Yara's boyfriend?

I wonder if Cole knows he's been relegated to the unnamed boyfriend.

"Hurry."

Raising his eyebrows at the prodding, Gray picked up the

pace through the restaurant to get outside. He found Cole standing with the twins and Yara at his back and a man who was clearly paparazzi in front of him.

Well, shit.

Gray turned to the side to tell the valet to call the police, for all the good it would do them. He'd yet to find a legal loophole to keep the papers away. *But first, the little fuckstick is going to get away from my kids.*

"Beard Guy." Alex waved cheerfully at him from behind Cole. He held up a piece of paper. "I sold the bike we built. Isn't it brilliant?"

Gray tried to stamp down the ridiculous sense of fatherly pride. His eyes stayed focused on the so-called journalist while he offered encouragement to Alex. "Good job. Why don't you head inside with your sister? I bet Yara can find some spare cake in the kitchen to celebrate."

"Cake!" Alex did a little dance before grabbing his sister and Yara by the hands to run toward the entrance to Ruck. "Cake. Cake. Cake. Cake."

Gray exchanged a smile with Cole. All of his friends and former co-workers had grown fond of Alice and Alex. His amusement disappeared immediately when the flash of a camera went off. "Can we *help* you?"

"Help? You want to help the fucker?" Cole teased him, earning a flick on the back of the head from Gray. "Jackass."

The journalist took a step forward, only to freeze when the attention of both retired military men turned toward him. "I'll tell the police you threatened me."

"And?" Gray moved up beside Cole. "Who do you think

they're likely to believe?"

"Me." The journalist didn't sound entirely confident.

"Yeah, and my dick's twenty inches long," Cole huffed.

"Do you roll it up to fit in your shorts?" Gray smirked at him. He feigned humour to remove some of the tension from the situation. "Typical SEAL, always exaggerating your abilities."

"Yeah, yeah, laugh it up, jarhead." Cole punched Gray lightly in the arm.

Before the paparazzo could respond, the police pulled into the parking lot. They swarmed forward to separate the three men. It didn't take long to explain the situation, and they thankfully escorted the journalist away—for the moment.

Cole followed him into Ruck once the police left. They found Alice, Alex, and Yara in the kitchen, eating leftover chocolate cake from the previous night. They'd made an impressive dent into it.

"All right, out of my kitchen, I have people to feed." Gray had to laugh when the twins took the platter with the cake with them. Cole followed them out with a fork in hand. "How many tables left to serve?"

"Five." Yara rushed over to wash her hands. "They're on the main course, at the moment. There's only the dessert to plate up in about ten minutes."

"Thanks." Gray nodded absently. He wondered how long it would take before those at the Sin Bin heard about the police presence. "Keep an eye out for Scottie or anyone from the club. Send them back to me."

"Sir, yes, sir." Yara grinned cheekily at him before dashing out of the kitchen.

"I feel old," Gray sighed. "Ancient."

"You are." Cole stepped back into the kitchen. "So, how's your new boy toy?"

Gray resisted the desire to snap at Cole. "It's not really any of your business, Voodoo. Is it?"

"I don't get it." Cole followed him across the kitchen toward the ovens. "Not judging you for your lifestyle, either."

Gray closed the oven door where he'd been checking on the last of the desserts for the evening menu. "Again, I say, it's none of your damn business."

"Fine." Cole stole a piece of potato from the sideboard. "Cagey old jarhead."

The influx of rugby players came after the desserts had been served. They had a lull of a few hours before set-up would begin for the evening reservations. He sipped coffee calmly while the group of friends peppered him with questions about the police presence.

"Bit anticlimactic," Scottie complained once Cole and Yara explained what happened, since Gray refused to answer. "Could've punched the fucking shit once for all the drama he started in the papers."

"Why? The paper has enough material on me without having photos of me pummelling a much smaller, younger man into the ground." Gray believed fully in deescalating any situation when possible. He'd learned over the years the power of remaining calm in the face of other people's anger and aggression. "It's time they focused on Ruck and the food—not the chef's private life."

"Fine," Scottie grumbled. "Fucking boring."

"Why don't I liven things up for us?" Gray had received a text invitation from Leo to the fire and ice event at the Red Card. "How much heat can you handle?"

"Whatever you can throw at me, old man." Scottie made it sound like a challenge.

"Careful, kitten." Gray lowered his voice so only his submissive could hear him. "You wouldn't want to start the evening already deserving punishment."

But I'd love it if you did.

The rest of his workday went smoothly. Gray managed to close up the restaurant in record time. He helped to clean up with an impatient Scottie waiting by the door.

As with all the other times they'd visited the BDSM club, a special room had been reserved for them. They found an outfit for Scottie laid out on the bed along with masks for both of them. Gray watched with eager anticipation while his submissive stripped down to nothing and slid into the leather straps.

"Come here, kitten." Gray stopped Scottie from buckling up the harness. He hooked a finger into one of the hooks to yank him closer. "We'll see how you can handle heat tonight."

Covering Scottie's mouth with his hand to stop him from speaking, Gray decided to insist on a *quiet* evening for his submissive. He provided him with a rubber ball to hold—and to drop if he wanted to stop play. Safe words sometimes required creativity.

Gray connected a lead to the ring that now sat at the base of Scottie's throat. He guided him out through the festively decorated first space deeper into the club. No need for an appetiser; their evening required more substance.

"Gandalf the Grey."

Gray wondered if he could separate the club from the owners. *Probably not.* "Run along and play with your own submissive, Leo."

"You'll find one of our playrooms all set up with the candles you prefer. All your special requests." Leo grinned wickedly from behind his devil mask. "Will you be putting on a show for yourself or for others to enjoy as well? You're such a possessive man. You rarely share your treasures with others."

Gray drew Scottie closer to his side while a group of men wandered by them. He narrowed his eyes on the still smirking Leo. "When was the last time you put Dimas on display?"

"Never fully."

"Precisely." Gray could count on one hand the number of times Leo had actually put on a demonstration with Dimas since they'd become serious about one another. "We had our exploration with putting him on display last time. If Scottie is interested, perhaps I'll allow you two to watch."

And he might.

Exhibitionism definitely tended to run hand in hand with many in the BDSM community. Gray for the most part preferred to keep complete control over who saw what. He trusted Leo and Dimas.

And that was about it.

"How about it, kitten?" Gray eased Scottie into one of the darkened corners for a private moment. "Want me to show them how wonderfully you submit?"

Scottie crossed his arms, getting the lead caught between them. "I'm not having the whole fucking club watch this time."

"Agreed. What about Leo and Dimas?" Gray placed the decision completely in his submissive's hands. "I can already see part of you is interested."

Scottie shifted slightly, which only made his growing erection stand out even more. "Fuck."

"Yes or no, boy. I won't decide for you." Gray tightened his grip on the leash. "Would you enjoy the heightened pleasure of knowing someone is watching your exquisite torture?"

"*Fuck*." Chapter Thirty-Three

Scottie

"I've died. Leave me to my misery." Scottie threw his arm over his eyes to block out the sudden brilliant light shining on his face. "You're a cruel bastard."

"So you said last night, but I'm not sure you meant it in the same way." Gray closed the curtains, shielding Scottie from the piercing brightness. "Out of bed, kitten. We're going to be late."

"Late? The fuck am I late for?"

Gray yanked the covers off Scottie. "Hamish convinced me to give a Range Rover a try. You're driving me over to pick one up. It's too damn cold to ride around on my bike all winter."

"Right."

Scrubbing his fingers across his face tiredly, Scottie tried to wake up. He'd gone deeply into subspace during their play at the Red Card. Gray always took good care of him afterwards, but it was difficult to get his mind back in gear.

His cock twitched a bit when he remembered being on display for Gray in one of the club's private rooms. They'd experimented with heat. He groaned in remembered pleasure and pain.

Stretched out on his back across a padded table that was covered with leather, Scottie had learned the joys of playing with heat. The club, to celebrate the theme of the evening, provided soy candles specifically designed for use in sex. Gray had clearly mastered the technique of tormenting him without the melted wax getting anywhere it shouldn't.

"Mind off your dick, kitten. Your body needs at least a day to recover," Gray warned sternly. Scottie knew he took the care of his submissive seriously. "If you can behave yourself, join me in the shower. Otherwise, you'll have to manage on your own."

With a regretful groan, Scottie rolled to the side of the bed and got to his feet. Gray threw an arm over his shoulder with a wry chuckle. *Fuck.* The deep laugh made Scottie feel as though someone had reached down to stroke a finger across his cock.

Bastard.

They showered slowly, enjoying the warmth of the hot water. November had turned bitterly cold, even for Cardiff. Scottie found himself uncharacteristically passive as Gray washed him, massaging away the aches in his slightly sore muscles.

The hot shower helped to bring Scottie back to himself.

He lounged around the kitchen while Gray made breakfast. *I'm going to need a shit tonne of coffee this morning.*

"You should move in with me." Gray spoke casually after they'd settled down to a simple omelette breakfast.

Scottie choked on a bite of toast. "Move in?"

Move in.

Can I live with someone without losing our minds or my temper?

Maybe with Gray.

Wait, does this mean he wants to—fuck no.

"I'm not marrying you." Scottie grabbed Gray's glass of juice to drink some to clear his throat. "Not interested in joint bank accounts and changing my name. All that useless shit married idiots do."

"Good. The only ring I'll put on you is one on your dick." Gray swatted Scottie's knuckles with his fork and took his cup back. "Are you opposed to the idea?"

"Are you actually asking me to shack up with you?" Scottie repeated the question rolling around in his mind. He did spend an increasing amount of time at the cottage and not in his own flat. "Seriously?"

"Don't believe I asked." Gray finished up his breakfast, grabbing the empty plates to head into the kitchen. "Think about it."

And Scottie did.

All day.

One of the bartenders at the Sin Bin eventually sent him to his office after he managed to dump a bucket of ice into a rubbish bin instead of the chest behind the bar. He sat at his desk and stared unseeing at the invoices in front of him. Gray's idea stayed at the forefront of his mind.

It wasn't the moving in part that bothered him. *Well, not just it.* In considering the idea, Scottie found a depth of emotions he'd been trying to avoid because of his lack of experience with them. It threw him off his normally confident stride.

Scottie looked up when someone knocked on the door. He told them to come in and found a familiar face stepping into his office. "Tens. What're you doing here without your nurse?"

"He's off somewhere with the non-profit he works for." Taine dropped into the chair across from Scottie. "Gina claims you've been a brainless zombie all day."

Scottie didn't think he'd been bad enough for his head bartender to complain to Taine. "A brainless zombie?"

"Her exact words. Did you really pour ice into the rubbish bin?" Taine plucked a bag of liquorice allsorts from his jacket pocket and tossed them over to him. "Remember when you insisted on eating half a bag before a match?"

Scottie opened the bag and dug around for one of the round pink candies. "We were a superstitious bunch of bastards."

Taine easily caught the candy cube thrown at him. "Do you want to talk about what has you so distracted?"

No.

Maybe.

"When you were a sprog, did your priest say he loved you?" Scottie found to his surprise and amusement that he'd managed to stun Taine. "Tens, speechless. BC owes me a fiver. We bet ages ago you'd never be completely lost for words."

Taine's rude gesture told Scottie exactly what he thought of the bet. "My adoptive father made a point to ensure I felt and understood I was loved and appreciated. I saw the evidence of parental love on a daily basis."

Twisting in his seat slightly, Scottie struggled to express his thoughts even to Taine, his one friend guaranteed not to tease him to death for showing his vulnerable side. He dug his fingers into the arm of his leather chair.

"Scottie?" Taine drew him away from the inspection of a loose thread on the chair. "Are you in love with Gray?"

"Don't be a twit," Scottie snapped sharply.

"Right." Taine raised his hands in an obvious effort to encourage him to maintain his calm. "Let's see if I can put your struggle into words. Your family raised you without even the façade of love. You've no idea how it feels, probably never heard anyone say it to you—outside of your friends or maybe Silus. You're emotionally stunted as a result. Before Gray, all romantic relationships were more one-night stand than long-term. Now you've gone and developed feelings for a bloke and have no clue how to handle them. Accurate summary?"

"Fuck off."

"So, that's a yes in Scottie speak." Taine blithely ignored Scottie's scowl. "The past can be an anchor to hold you in one spot forever, or you can use it as fuel to drive you into a happier future. Your father's dead. He can't hurt you anymore unless you give his ghost the power to do so. Move on. Acknowledge that the Monk family, in general, are shitty people, you and Silus aside. Don't screw up your happiness because they're all miserable arseholes."

Scottie took a moment to process the forceful speech Taine had unloaded on him. "How long have you been holding all that in?"

"Ages. Since it became clear Gray had become a fixture in your life. Just think about it." Taine stretched an arm out to nick another candy from the bag. "The party started an hour ago. You're late for it."

"Fuck." Scottie dropped the liquorice on his desk. "You couldn't have mentioned that at the start?"

Kicking his friend out of his office, Scottie changed quickly into the 1920s gangster suit one of the staff had picked up for him for the fancy dress party. He'd promised to make an appearance during the event. All of the owners had agreed to it for the publicity, part of why they'd been in town to stage their little intervention.

The pinstriped suit fit him perfectly. Scottie stepped into the employee loo to get a quick peek in the mirror. *Not bad.* He went down to check with both his bartenders and the doorman to ensure everything had started smoothly.

Scottie almost walked into one of the pillars when he spotted Gray in what had to be his old uniform. "Fuck me."

His Dominant strode confidently through the crowd. Scottie couldn't resist a smirk when Gray appeared just as affected by his suit. He owed Gina a bonus for picking it out for him.

"Am I going to need to wear this next time we play?" Gray's dark tone drifted along Scottie's spine like fingertips. "Careful, kitten. We don't want everyone to see how hard you are for me. Not sure you want that amount of attention in your club."

His cock was rock-hard for Gray, no point in denying it. The vision of submitting for him while in his uniform made Scottie almost light-headed with desire. He contemplated ducking into his office for a quick wank to release the pressure.

"Patience." Gray stopped him with a hard glance. "Enjoy the party. Your dick can wait."

No, it can't.

Bastard.

CHAPTER THIRTY-FOUR

GRAY

December started with an early winter snow. It never seemed to end, with January bringing even more of the fluffy white stuff. The blanket of it was pretty—especially since Gray didn't have to get out into it.

Never prone to looking backward, Gray oddly found himself thinking back to the previous year when he'd spent Christmas with Scottie and the twins. It had been the start of their relationship in many ways. He thought it seemed ages ago—not just twelve months.

After a massive holiday rush of reservations, Ruck had been closed for a two-week break. Gray planned to enjoy the most of it. He didn't expect his cottage to be invaded almost every day by Alice and Alex.

"What the fuck are they doing?" Scottie joined him at

the living room window looking out over the front garden. "They'll freeze their fingers off."

"They're attempting to create a snow biker. They made their family of snowmen in the backyard. Now it's time for something new in the front." Gray had allowed the twins to borrow a spare jacket and helmet—both had been damaged, so a little snow wouldn't do further harm. "Alex's idea."

"Naturally." Scottie laughed before handing a cup of coffee to Gray. He took a sip from his own mug. "Silus and Zippie are going to help me sort out the rest of my stuff next week. They should be back from Portsmouth after spending the holidays with Remi and Sarah."

After over a month of thinking about it, Scottie had decided to give his flat to his brother. Silus initially refused, but after a third break-in at his own place he'd changed his mind. With most of the furniture staying in the apartment, it wouldn't take much to get Scottie completely moved out.

And in with me.

Not that we haven't been living together for months anyway.

Gray turned his attention away from the frolicking autistic twins to a box sitting on the mantle over the fireplace. He'd set it there a few weeks ago, teasing Scottie, who wanted to know what it was. "Get the present, kitten."

"What?" Scottie slowly pulled his gaze away from the window to follow Gray's pointing finger toward the fireplace. "Ah. Now? You've made me wait how long?"

Gray took the box from Scottie when he retrieved it. "You'll learn patience, kitten, one way or the other."

"Bastard."

"Yes." Gray discarded the top of the box and allowed Scottie to see the bracelet inside. "You'll note the clear absence of a ring."

The bracelet was made out of surgical stainless steel and shaped as a handcuff. Subtle enough not to disturb anyone who might be offended by alternative lifestyles, the cuff fit perfectly around Scottie's wrist. Gray secured it, running his fingers along his submissive's wrist.

They'd discussed a variety of ways to declare their relationship, including a bracelet. Gray had never been fond of permanent methods—tattoos or piercings. He'd known a number of both submissives and Dominants who'd deeply regretted getting an inked reminder.

"*Mine*." Gray tugged hard on the bracelet. "If we didn't have visitors, you'd be on your knees showing your appreciation for my gift."

"Just send their arses home." He shifted his body forward as if wanting to drop to the floor. "They can walk. Or crawl."

"And get lost in a snowdrift?"

"Character building. Isn't that what you marine bastards call it?" Scottie dropped a hand down to tug on his shaft through his trousers. "Someone'll pick them up."

"*Kitten*." Gray shook his head at Scottie.

"Fine." Scottie glared at him before turning to head toward the door. "Well, if I'm not getting a good fuck, might as well freeze my arse off with them."

Resigning himself to a day in the cold, Gray followed Scottie outside. The twins seemed surprised and excited to see them. Their snowcycle appeared a bit more like molten plastic than anything else.

Scottie solved the problem by tackling Gray into the lopsided sculpture. Alice and Alex stared at them for a second before pelting them both with snowballs. *I'm too fucking old to fight in the cold. But if they start it, I'm going to win.*

"You're taking fire."

Gray glanced up from where he'd crouched behind his new SUV to find Aled and Wyatt watching him. "They decided to gang up on me."

"Tactical retreat?" Wyatt snickered at him. "Aren't you jarheads supposed to be made of sterner stuff?"

"Going to help me, or do you plan on talking shit?" Gray peeked around the edge of the vehicle to see if any of his three opponents had snuck up on him. "You're giving away my position."

Wyatt put two fingers in his mouth to whistle sharply. "Hey, blond squared. He's over here."

"Earp?"

Wyatt glanced over as Gray got to his feet. "Yes?"

"*Run.*"

With Aled snickering behind them, Gray took off after his old Navy SEAL buddy. Wyatt dodged and weaved, trying to use anything at his disposal to block Gray's path. He caught up to him, sweeping his legs to knock Wyatt face first into the snow.

He came up spluttering with a snow beard. "Dickhead."

"No one likes a whiner, Earp." Gray kicked snow at him. "Fuck it's cold out here. Time to head inside before we run the risk of losing our fingers."

Inviting Wyatt and his husband to join them, Gray threw another log on the fire. He moved into the kitchen to get some hot chocolate going. The Brits might want tea, but he preferred a rare sweet treat to warm up his insides.

"Saw the bracelet."

Gray ignored Wyatt, who'd followed him into the kitchen. "Coffee, tea, or hot chocolate?"

"I saw the bracelet."

"I heard you. I simply chose to ignore you since it's none of your damn business." Gray got the milk going on the stove for the hot chocolate. "I can feel you glaring—stop before I give in to my urge to dig your eyes out with a spoon."

"You'd try." Wyatt leaned against the counter, reaching out to steal a piece of chocolate. He yanked it back when Gray smacked his knuckles with a wooden spoon.

Gray decided to deflect the conversation about his relationship before it could start. "How was France?"

For the holidays, Wyatt had taken his husband to France to see his parents. The twins had been in and out checking all of Aled's precious plants for him. He figured the trip would be a safer topic for them than his relationship.

"It was French." Wyatt shrugged. "Did you know Voodoo introduced Yara to his parents?"

"I did." Gray tensed, waiting for what Wyatt had to say next. "I haven't seen either of them with Ruck closed for vacation. Yara texted Alice to say it went and I quote, 'so brilliantly, his mum's a gem.'"

"I hope you appreciate my efforts in bringing all of you

to a place where you could find love. You'd all be sad and lonely without me." Wyatt managed to steal another piece of chocolate while Gray focused on finding enough mugs. "Going to say thank you?"

Deciding the question didn't deserve an answer, Gray ignored it. He had to guard the rest of the chocolate against the invading SEAL. They eventually managed to get warm drinks ready.

True to form, Alice and Alex took their hot chocolates down the hall. Gray had set up one of the guest rooms into a quiet space for them. Among other things, it had bunk beds for them to sleep in if they stayed over.

Aled slid across the couch to sit closer to Gray while Wyatt and Scottie started an argument about rugby and American football. "They talk about you."

"Your plants?" Gray couldn't help teasing.

"Americans. Always with the jokes." Aled brought his legs up to sit cross-legged on the couch. They'd all abandoned their damp shoes by the door. "The twins. You've been more of a father to them than anyone else. Alex always talks about how much you've taught him about engines."

Gray kept an eye on Scottie and Wyatt, knowing the debate could get unnecessarily heated. "They're good kids."

"Agreed." Aled nodded. "But, you're a good man, as well."

Trying to deflect the conversation with a shrug, Gray shifted the topic to how Aled's plants were handling the frigid temperatures. Botany went right over his head. He tried to appear at least mildly interested since he'd been the one to ask in the first place.

"Beard guy?"

Gray sent a glare at Wyatt for snickering at the nickname before turning to find Alex hovering by the end of the hallway. "More hot chocolate?"

"Not more chocolate." Alex drew patterns in the air with his fingers repeatedly. "My class next week has a family day."

Seeing how nervous Alex was, Gray tried to smile encouragingly when his courage clearly faltered. Alice rushed up to join her brother. She hovered beside him without touching him.

"Doyouwanttocome?" Alex asked, speaking so fast the words blended together. "Please?"

Aled sent a pointed look toward Gray as if to say "what did I tell you."

Gray ignored him, focusing on Alex who seemed to have stopped breathing while waiting for an answer. "Of course, I'll be there. Just tell me when and where."

"Oh, good. You said yes." Alex beamed brightly at him before rushing away, flapping his hands excitedly.

Family is what you make of it.

Gray stretched his legs out in front of the fire to warm up his toes more. "Are you two staying for lunch?"

"Have I ever turned down a free meal?" Wyatt slipped his arm around his husband's shoulders to draw him closer. "Besides, I'm not going outside until my socks are dry."

"Shouldn't a Navy SEAL be less affected by dampness?" Aled smiled up at Wyatt, who tugged on his long hair in retaliation. "Can we help with fixing the meal?"

"Not if he wants it to taste even remotely edible."

"I'm not *that* bad." Aled threatened his husband with his teaspoon. "I order takeaways brilliantly."

With the twins hiding out with their music to relax after a morning of being social, Gray continued to enjoy the warmth of the fire. His plans for lunch required a minimal amount of work. He hadn't intended to have four extra guests, but it didn't really matter.

"Why the hell do people have kids?" Scottie asked out of nowhere. His fingers wrapped tightly around his mug. "Got fucking frostbite playing with those two."

Gray watched Scottie out of half-closed eyes. "I'll see if I can't warm you up a bit later."

"We're still in the damn room." Wyatt threw a damp sock at Gray's head. "Keep it in your pants, marine."

"My house. My pants. My fucking room." Gray caught Scottie by the collar of his T-shirt to drag him over into a hard kiss. "You can always leave."

"What? And miss dinner and a show?" Wyatt applauded. "Encore."

"I'll encore you upside the head. Get your ass in the kitchen. You can peel potatoes for me." Gray released Scottie and slowly stood up. He snapped his fingers at Wyatt, who saluted him. "That's what I like to see—respect."

"Yeah, only because you're older than Methuselah." Wyatt trotted after him into the kitchen. "I haven't peeled a potato in years."

Gray set several of them on the counter. "Here's your chance to practice."

"Don't you have a slave to handle this?"

Gray carefully set the carton of eggs on the counter before turning to address the slightly flippant remark. "A submissive is *not* a slave."

"Just a joke."

He narrowed his eyes on Wyatt. "Behave yourself, Earp. I'd hate to demonstrate how easily I can kick your ass in front of your husband."

CHAPTER THIRTY-FIVE

SCOTTIE

By the first rains of spring, Scottie had gotten comfortable living in the cottage. His brother had tried to pay rent, grumbling when he ignored the offer. Silus being situated in a decent flat made him happy.

Made Silus's mum happy as well, until they both realised Zeb planned to live with him. Scottie wanted to have a few words, maybe more than words, with him. Gray reminded him it would be slightly hypocritical.

Slightly.

Zeb and Silus were both old enough to make their own decisions. Scottie knew his brother tended to be more mature than he'd been at his age. They'd be fine.

He hoped. Remi wouldn't appreciate it if his younger cousin wound up in a hospital. Scottie took the care of his sibling seriously.

In the months since his breakdown after the funeral, Scottie had worked hard at dealing with his anger. He didn't want to fall apart anytime something difficult happened. His father had provided a living example of where that road ended.

His rehab sponsor had challenged him to do more for others. Silus suggested it meant he should "stop being such a selfish arsehole." A bit rich coming from his brother who currently lived rent-free in his old flat.

Sobriety hadn't changed his personality. Scottie did, however, see the point of perhaps stepping outside of himself. He spent several weeks considering what he might do.

In the end, Gray provided the best idea. He'd suggested Scottie find a way to help kids who'd grown up similarly to himself. They'd both experienced how an abusive home could impact a child's life long into adulthood.

A brilliant idea.

His only problem came from his being too lazy to run his own charity or find one to work with on his own. Scottie pressed his tech-savvy brother into doing the research for him. They eventually found a Cardiff non-profit that worked specifically with at-risk youths from troubled homes.

The first meeting with the youngsters, who ranged in age from eight to eighteen, left him greatly humbled. Scottie listened to their stories; many were worse than his own. He suddenly could understand more clearly what made Gray give so freely of himself to Alice and Alex.

Like him, most of the kids had no one standing in their corner, offering encouragement and safety. Scottie didn't quite know how much of a difference his presence made. He hoped if nothing else, the world seemed a bit less bleak.

He'd come a long way from the battered boy who stumbled onto a rugby pitch.

He was proud of himself.

In the midst of all of this, Scottie had gotten a call from the caretaker at the cemetery. They'd had a bit of trouble. He steeled himself to deal with yet another drama indirectly related to his father.

"I'd hoped to never have to come here again." Scottie grimaced at the new stone marking his dad's grave. "Well, I don't feel like taking a piss on it—so that's something."

Vandals had ruined several gravestones in the cemetery. Scottie had commissioned the new one and come out to see it with Gray. Silus had picked out the design for both of them, while he paid for it.

Gray stood beside him, offering silent support, as he'd done throughout everything. "Not sure the caretakers would appreciate you urinating on a grave, even if your old man deserved it."

"Could spit on it." Scottie considered it seriously but instead turned his back on the name in granite mocking him. "That's my good deed done."

"For the week?"

"For the rest of my fucking life," Scottie snorted in slightly bitter amusement. "I repaid his abuse with kindness by paying his hospital bills, covering his funeral, and ensuring a decent memorial to his name. It's enough."

"You didn't owe him a thing." Gray followed him down

the winding path. "You didn't do it for him in any case."

"Or for me." Scottie paused with his hands on the gate leading to the car park. "I did it for Silus. If I hadn't, he would've emptied his bank account to care for our old man. In the end, his heart would've been broken by our dad's bitterness while his little bit of money evaporated into nothing."

The majority of his rare moments of selflessness generally revolved around Silus. His brother brought out the best in him. The gravestone had been yet another example of it.

"I'm proud of you." Gray dropped a hand onto his shoulder, pushing him through the gate toward the Jaguar. "Would you like a treat, kitten?"

"You're a fucking arsehole." Scottie scowled at him—more annoyed with his instant reaction to the tone in his Dominant's voice. "Yes, I would."

Gray chuckled darkly at the admission. "Poor boy. I'll drive. You're going to be too busy to focus on road safety."

Fuck me.

I'm already fucking hard.

And Gray ensured Scottie stayed hard for the next few hours.

In the car, in the kitchen, and finally in the back garden.

On his hands and knees, hidden by the tall hedges, Scottie didn't quite remember how they'd gone from the vehicle through the house and finally outside. The ring around his cock stopping his release held almost all of his attention. Gray's cock had the rest of his focus as it slid in and out of him.

They eventually collapsed on the grass, completely spent,

to stare up at the fluffy clouds drifting by while trying to catch their breaths. Scottie thought they'd need to move inside soon even if their sides were pressed together. It was still too early in the year to be starkers outside for too long.

The comfortable silence between them drew Scottie's thoughts away from his pleasurably sore body to other thoughts. He'd found submission often cleared his mind in a way nothing else ever had. *Not that I'll ever admit it to anyone—other than Gray.*

His thoughts inevitably turned to his father and the family legacy. In many ways, Scottie had broken the cycle of drinking and violence. At times, he might still struggle with wanting a drink or losing his temper, but overall, he'd grown up.

He hoped his courage to change ensured Silus never fell into many of the same traps. His brother had had a better start than he did. It didn't mean Monk blood didn't run in his veins.

Nature versus nurture?

His therapist had a lot to say on the topic. Scottie didn't quite believe in all the philosophical nonsense. He couldn't deny his childhood had greatly affected him, so perhaps it was a bit of both.

The words stayed with him long after the bruises had faded, all of the words his father had flung at him, sharp enough to leave him bleeding as if struck by a knife. Scottie had often used whisky to drown all of it out.

"He was wrong."

"Who?" Gray lifted his head up off the grass to glance over at him. "Wrong about what?"

"My old man." Scottie toyed with the bracelet on his wrist.

He'd been surprised at first when Gray mentioned getting him one. The more he'd thought about it, the more he looked forward to having the constant physical reminder of their connection. "Bastard said I've never amount to anything, and I'd die miserably without anyone to mourn me."

"Sounds more like what happened to him," Gray remarked.

"I made something of myself. Might've fucked up a time or two, but I didn't wind up living in a cardboard box, drunk off my arse." Scottie dropped his fingers from his wrist to rest on Gray's forearm. "Not miserable or alone—not anymore."

Not ever again.

ACKNOWLEDGEMENTS

A massive thank you to my betas, Becky, Olivia and all the brilliant people at Hot Tree, and my beloved hubby.

Thanks to all of my readers, whether this is the first or sixth of my stories that you've read. I'm so glad you enjoy the crazy lives of the lads of The Sin Bin as much as I do.

ABOUT THE AUTHOR

Dahlia Donovan wrote her first romance series after a crazy dream about shifters and damsels in distress. She prefers irreverent humour and unconventional characters.

An autistic and occasional hermit, her life wouldn't be complete without her husband and her massive collection of books and video games.

Stay connected with Dahlia:

Facebook: www.facebook.com/dahliadonovan

Website: http://dahliadonovan.com

Twitter: https://twitter.com/DahliaDonovan

If you enjoyed reading this book, please consider leaving a review.

ABOUT THE PUBLISHER

Hot Tree Publishing opened its doors in 2015 with an aspiration to bring quality fiction to the world of readers. With the initial focus on romance and a wide spread of romance sub-genres, we envision opening to alternative genres in the near future.

Firmly seated in the industry as a leading editing provider to independent authors and small publishing houses, Hot Tree Publishing is the sister company to Hot Tree Editing, founded in 2012. Having established in-house editing and promotions, plus having a well-respected market presence, Hot Tree Publishing endeavours to be a leader in bringing quality stories to the world of readers.

Interested in discovering more amazing reads brought to you by Hot Tree Publishing? Head over to the website for more:

WWW.HOTTREEPUBLISHING.COM